THE GUN ROOM

THE GUN ROOM

GEORGINA HARDING

BLOOMSBURY

NEW YORK · LONDON · OXFORD · NEW DELHI · SYDNEY

Bloomsbury USA

An imprint of Bloomsbury Publishing Plc

1385 Broadway	50 Bedford Square
New York	London
NY 10018	WC1B 3DP
USA	UK

www.bloomsbury.com

BLOOMSBURY and the Diana logo are trademarks of Bloomsbury Publishing Plc

First published in Great Britain 2016

First U.S. edition 2016

ISBN:	HB:	978-1-63286-436-9
	ePub:	978-1-63286-438-3

Library of Congress Cataloging-in-Publication Data is available.

2 4 6 8 10 9 7 5 3 1

Typeset by Integra Software Services Pvt. Ltd.
Printed and bound in USA by Berryville Graphics Inc., Berryville, Virginia

To find out more about our authors and books visit www.bloomsbury.com.
Here you will find extracts, author interviews, details of forthcoming events, and
the option to sign up for our newsletters.

Bloomsbury books may be purchased for business or promotional use. For information
on bulk purchases please contact Macmillan Corporate and Premium Sales Department
at specialmarkets@macmillan.com.

'[Photographs] are the proof that something was there and no longer is. Like a stain.'

Diane Arbus

1
Soldier

It is the eyes that make the picture great. The soldier's eyes look out directly from the page. They look out and through – or perhaps they are not looking at all but seeing only what they have seen already, images that are imprinted on the retina and on the memory so strongly that they cannot be supplanted by whatever is before them now. This soldier has seen horrors first hand. Perhaps he has been a perpetrator of them? The viewer can only imagine, from experience perhaps but more likely from things that he or she has read and other photographs that he or she has seen, and imagines now, cumulatively, knowing and having seen those things, and seeing the photograph and the look in the soldier's eyes. This may be one of the great photographs of the war; the sort of photograph that might have made its photographer famous, if he had not fled.

From the air, the landscape was awash with mist. Hills floated above it, inky jungle ridges and sometimes the crowns of individual trees, but the mist lay wide and deep where the land flattened into delta. In the far distance, a white disc of sun lit a silver brushstroke of sea. It was an oriental scroll unrolled beneath him, an exotic floating world to which he had no connection. His existence was all within the hard bubble of the chopper, a glass-and-metal bubble of noise and vibration and shouted words. He couldn't make out the half of what was said but he nodded and mouthed back, and bent past the machine-gunner in the doorway and took pictures of the mist breaking, the paddy beginning to show, and colour – bright green squares, red-earth tracks, already-warm blue sky, and somewhere away across the fields, a dark billowing in the air that could not be mist, to which he saw the pilot was pointing.

He had met the pilot in a bar the night before, a young American flyer no older than himself. His name was Jeff. They had got on well. They had gone outside into the night and smoked some weed. He had said he was a freelance though he was barely even that, and Jeff had offered the ride just to show him the sights. He hadn't promised any action. Whatever it was Jeff shouted now he couldn't hear, as the chopper turned and headed towards the smoke. He guessed it was something to do with luck. He was excited with his first-timer's luck.

The village was some way off. They flew over fields where people were working, so low that he could see their conical bamboo hats and their heads turning towards the chopper, and some of the people running, not knowing that they did not mean to shoot. Indian country, Jeff yelled then, as if these were Apache below, but he got the point. Any of these people might be regarded as hostile. They flew over lines of craters that showed where others had flown before, craters in the irrigated fields gleaming with water that reflected the chopper passing, others in the jungle that were just brick-red holes, or sometimes the red ringed with black from incendiaries. You could see how the bombs had dropped, one after the other, across the land. But he wasn't taking pictures now. He did not intend to waste his film on landscape. He didn't even take a picture of the first action that he saw, the first live piece of war that he had ever seen. They were just coming to the village, low, wheeling round, looking for a place to land. There was a woman wounded, lying across one of the paths in the paddy. They were so low that they could see her spread hair and her splayed legs in the black trousers, and her tunic thrown up, and see that she was young and that she was screaming, and clearly see that she had some wound on her middle where her hands clutched. Jeff went lower and the gunner dropped a flare to mark her for the medics. As the chopper moved away he thought he saw a soldier running to where she was and firing at her head. He saw it only out of the corner of his eye, looking back, his view restricted, and then he wondered if that could really be what he had seen. It happened so fast, and the chopper moved on and landed, and then he was out of it, and there was so much else going on.

He had the camera about his neck. He was running, crouched, holding the camera. The rotor blades were still turning overhead, blasting hot air and dust against his face, throwing down the long grass through which he ran and driving it outwards in waves. There was the heat and the smoke and the fire-and-metal smell of the place, but the sound of it came to him only as the chopper engine stilled. The sound was more like a wind than anything that he had expected of war, a wind and a wildfire, a sound that seemed made all of movement and burning and yet a part of it came from within himself. No explosions. No gunshots. Was there danger? He didn't know. He had expected to dodge, but there was nothing to dodge, only a line to walk towards the centre of the smoke and the sound, to where the shooting must so short a time before have taken place. He was in luck, Jeff had said. He would see action. But he was behind the action. The shooting was over. He was late. He was a moment too late and he was walking not into action but into the aftermath of action, into the rushing and the smoke, and he could not have told how fast he walked because time seemed to have split between himself and the commotion there ahead of him, as if he was in one time and that was in another. And then he saw the soldier, and he could not have said to which time the soldier belonged. The soldier was still. He was seated on the ground with his back to a wall, his back to all of that. The soldier was sitting very still and straight, with his knees bent up in front of him and his two hands clamped to the barrel of the gun held upright between them. He noticed the soldier because he sat so still, and because his features were so clean and strong, almost heroic. He stopped and took a first picture of him as he passed.

Beyond the soldier, the village. The houses were burning. Bright flames leapt within doors and windows. Thick smoke seeped and clung and then poured from thatch, seething along the ground as well as into the sky as if it was too heavy to rise, melded and weighted there with the churned dust, and through that smoke and dust figures milled as senselessly as the smoke, villagers and soldiers, and small scared black pigs like squealing demons at their feet. Everything seemed to continue in motion though the cause of the motion was past. Even the dead, when he came to them, seemed caught in the act of moving. An old man running with his arm outstretched as if to catch his flyaway hat a yard from his fingers. A boy and a dog tumbled over one another as if in play. He took these pictures and he took others, those more predictable ones of confusion in the smoke. Hectic images they would be, of erratic depth and focus: crumpled figures on the ground with their limbs bared and askew, dead and living faces smeared with dust and blood, men with guns and women with their hands in the air, a grandmother whose grief broke her face wide open.

He would have taken more. He would not have known where to stop. He went to the side of one building that was not burning and fumbled to change a roll of film. His hands were clumsy, not his own. So much less control he had of those awkward sweating hands than of the black mechanism of the camera. He had no thought. He was not even hearing the sound of the place now. He had only eyes, only a sense of the images: that there were more, that images were disappearing with every second that he wasted.

Then he stumbled round the corner of the building and found himself at the end of the village. He had walked through it and suddenly it was behind him, at his back.

He could hear it and he could smell it but it was behind him, and before him were the fields, so green and still. The rush left him and self-awareness returned. He took a couple of steps out into the green. He turned and took some shots looking back at the village, shots that would establish the reality of it among the fields. Turning again, he looked at the ground at his feet, the young rice about him, the fields that ran to the flat horizon; this place where he was. There was a separation in his mind between here where he was and the burning village, this moment now and the ones before. Yet there in the village too it would be slowing now, since there were no shots to be heard. The dust would be beginning to settle, the smoke to rise, the dead to look dead. He walked on a little way, walked on along a dyke with that separation in his head, and then he looked down into the irrigation channel beside it and there were dead people in the channel. Here, now, in this place also, the reality. Half submerged in the murky water of the channel were the bodies of four or five men scrambled together. He took pictures but even in the pictures the number would not be clear, the arms and legs so scrambled, heads lost in the water. He could not tell if they had been tipped there or if they had been killed on the dyke and fallen, or maybe they had been shot from above, by someone standing where he stood, as they tried to hide. Someone standing on that spot, looking down and killing in cold blood.

And then he remembered the woman. He looked across all the fields trying to get his bearings, though the land was flat and the paddy looked much the same all round the village. Again he looked back at the village itself. He thought that he knew the way the chopper had come, thought he recognised a grove of mango trees and a particular configuration of palms. He was moving slowly now, thoughtful, deliberate. He was beginning to understand what it was that he was seeing. He headed in the direction of the palms, but indirectly as many of the fields were flooded and he had to walk along the edges of first one and then another on the narrow raised paths that bordered them – slow paths, he saw they were, paths that were made not to be walked fast or directly by rushing men with guns or cameras, but to be padded barefoot and single file by peasants in the patience of a peasant day. He let the camera drop loose from his neck. He was shaking. Now that he had slowed he realised that he was shaking, and he was aware of time and looked at his watch, and saw that he should get back to the chopper. Forty-five minutes, Jeff had said. Already he had been gone that. He told himself that he must find the chopper. He could not be left here in Indian country. And he was just about to turn back when he saw her. She was in that same position across the path as he had seen her before from the air, but limp, not taut any more, the same black hair, the black trousers, the black tunic thrown back, the wound gaping red on her belly, but a second wound now precise on her forehead and a crimson pool beneath her darkening the orange soil. About her were the signs of her interrupted work: a hat and a hoe, and a piece of turquoise cloth of the type in which a baby

9

would have been carried, snaking down from the path into the flooded field. He looked around but he couldn't see any baby. He took a picture – though the light by now made it flat and it wasn't a great picture – and then he walked back to where the chopper waited, knowing his way because this was the way they had flown in overhead so short a time before.

Again the soldier was there by the wall. A second time, he stopped to photograph him. Even now it was hard to keep from shaking so it seemed to take a long time to compose the shot. He could see the chopper. The chopper was starting up. But the chopper could see him and the chopper must wait. This picture he knew he must have. He knew, as if from deep inside himself, the look in the soldier's eyes. Or that look touched him deep inside. He took a breath from there, from the depths, and when he had the shaking under control he went in close and crouched down low. The soldier did not move. The soldier did not appear to see him. He made the shot entirely symmetrical, centred on the vertical of the gun barrel and the unseeing eyes. He composed it so tightly that when it was eventually published it was not cropped at all. His lens captured every detail: the coating of dust on the soldier's skin and his fingers, the contrasting sheen of the gun metal, the bristle of beard on him, the slightly open lips, the shadow of his helmet that fell across his face above his staring eyes. And when, months afterwards, he compared this shot with the first that he had taken, he realised that the soldier could not have moved in all the time he had been

in the village. Or perhaps he had blinked. He must have blinked. He had shot the first picture head-on as this one, but from a slightly different level, looking downwards, and from a greater distance so that there was more to the fore and to the sides – a dusty space in front, a section of mud wall to the soldier's right, a distracting sliver of smoke and activity to the left – but the central image was identical.

That evening he went out with Jeff. That was a bad one, Jeff said. That was all he said about the day. The day was put away. They had landed at the airstrip, and stepped out and down onto tarmac, and there were American voices all round them and it had seemed like a hot and scented version of America, and later the night had fallen, very suddenly, and they went out from the base to a bar on the shanty strip beyond the gates. Jeff wanted to get blasted. They had a few drinks first out in the street, and then they went inside. The Happiness Bar, the place was called, with pink and green and yellow lights strung outside of it like a fairground. There was the Fanny Bar next door, and the Sexy Snack, but Jeff had a regular girl at the Happiness.

She has a friend, Jeff said. He asked the girl, Do you have a friend for my friend?

The girl was little, but all of them were little beside the Americans. She seemed pretty, as so many of them were, young and delicately formed, but in the dimness of the bar

he could see little more than black hair and bright lipstick, and the flirtatious upturn of her face. He guessed that her friend when she came would look much the same, and he was right.

My name Dolly. What your name?

Was that a name in Vietnamese? He didn't know any girls' names in Vietnamese.

Jonathan, he said.

She repeated his name. It was an alien language, Vietnamese, made up of multiple tones. When they spoke English it sounded mechanical. They sounded mechanical.

It was too hot in the bar, the space so cramped that the air from the fan was blocked by the bodies in front of it. They took their drinks and the girls out into the street where it was cooler and the night when you looked away from the lights was almost blue. He was drunk and stoned, and for a moment he thought Dolly was actually beautiful beneath the pink and green and yellow lights. He looked at her, and he tried not to look at anything that was inside himself. That made him reel, to look into himself; if he did that he was lost. So he stood his ground and looked at Dolly, if that was her name. He saw that she was fine-boned, her hands small and finely made and elegant. She had a lovely exotic way of holding them. They dance with their hands here, he thought, seeing the way her fingers with their tapering pink-painted nails held a cigarette. They ended up in a lean-to at the side of the Happiness. One of the lights hung just outside the window, a yellow one.

He saw that it wasn't a coloured bulb, only a plain one with yellow tissue paper wrapped about it – that might catch fire, you would think, only it didn't, or hadn't yet. He was trivially aware of that, and of the girl's face in the yellow light that came through the window, and the shape of her cheekbones and the slanting shadows of her eyes beneath him, and at the same time there was the other one, the woman on the path.

You different. Why you different?

Not a soldier. The words seemed apart from him, carrying no significance. Not American. English.

He had closed his eyes but now he opened them again. Her face was yellow below him, her hair black, her eyes deep shadows. He saw that woman flat on the narrow path and the red on her belly. Dolly's skin beneath him was unbroken, smooth, the colour of marzipan in that light. He could not touch it.

He went back to his hotel. He didn't sleep but packed his things, not telling himself what he was doing but just doing it, as if his body acted independently from himself. He hitched a ride out on the back of a jeep before he had to speak to anyone. He didn't want to encounter anyone who knew about the day before. He had taken the films from that day and packed them inside his socks at the bottom of his rucksack, not with the others in the camera bag. He didn't know yet where to use them, if he would use them. In the light of another dawn, with the next dawn's low mist over the land, only the sickness he felt inside him made him believe that they were there and that they contained the images they contained. The road ran along a dyke, raised above the fields. As the mist cleared along the road, white strands clung below. Already people were at work in the fields, where sections were flooded for planting, groups of squatting black figures planting out green shoots of rice. These fields and figures were identical to yesterday's. As if there was no war. He held on to the metal bar at the back of the jeep and looked down at them along the receding line of the road. There were the bright squares thick with seedling rice. They took the shoots from the squares in bundles and planted them out in the irrigated beds, squatting, moving forward, inserting the shoots one by one, in lines and precisely spaced. He knew that here they had two, maybe three, crops of rice in a year. Two or three times a year the cycle was patiently repeated, this planting in the wet, harvesting, planting. As if that was all there ever had been or should be. He could not bear what he was, moving away so fast in the jeep.

He didn't go out to the countryside again. He spent the rest of his time in Saigon. There were others there like himself, besides the professionals, young men, even a few women, who'd made their way in somehow and were working at being reporters or photo-journalists, or just war groupies having adventures or maybe doing business, importing jukeboxes or Levi's. They were loud. They drank a lot. They thought that being in Vietnam was exhilarating yet a lot of the time they just hung out at the hotel. From the hotel roof they could see the smoke of distant air strikes. He had read his Hemingway too. A writer was forged in war,

14

Hemingway had said. A photographer, more so. He had talked his way out there like they had, with toughness and dreams, but he didn't want to drink with them any more. He left the hotel in the morning before most of them were up, and went out and took pictures on the streets, of girls and bicycles and street sellers and cafes with bamboo chairs outside, that were all the more photogenic because you knew about the war being out there in the jungle and the paddy, and suspected that sometime not too far off it would be here in the city as well, and all this would come to an end. At five o'clock in the afternoons he went downtown to the daily press briefing. He got into the habit of this. He'd gone to the press briefing the day he came back on the jeep, to see if they said anything about the attack on the village, but they didn't, and he got to going every day just in case he heard the place mentioned, some official tone putting an acceptable reality, or at least a narrative, to what he thought he had seen. Otherwise he tried to put it out of his mind. That didn't work, of course. He knew the truth and he knew that he should have been telling it. The truth lay there all the time, like the rolls of film in those socks that he didn't wear in the heat, in the bottom of his rucksack in the bare hot room that he didn't visit all day, that he slept in so fitfully at night.

It was only much later, when he was out of the country and the pictures were developed, that he had the contact sheets before him and saw plainly what he taken, frame by frame.

When his thirty-day visa ran out he went to Hong Kong. He didn't try to renew but got some commercial work there. He had a few introductions. He found a tiny room at the back of someone's nice apartment on the Island with a slice of view down and across to Kowloon. The expat world was easy. It was easy, if you were British, to find work and an air-conditioned room and go out to eat exotically in the evening among the sampans in the harbour. He might have stayed much longer. But then he heard the name of the village in the news. It was named as the site of some atrocity.

He took the films for processing, and when the contacts were done he stayed in the shop to look at them. He asked for a magnifying glass and a china marker, took the glossy black-and-white sheets from their envelope and went through them then and there, where there was a lamp at a cramped table alongside the counter. He knew that it was best to do the job there, functionally, in that tight bare professional space where people shouted over his bent head in Chinese and did not know the meaning of what he did. He worked swiftly, because they were impatient with him in the shop but also because he could not allow himself thought. He would be professional as he had been at the time, when he had the lens between himself and what he saw. Alone before those images he would have been naked. He bent over the table and adjusted the lamp, moved the glass methodically along and down each sheet. One 35mm frame, one instant. And then the next. Beneath the glass the instants grew and massed one upon another. That was how they occurred, how it had been, but he tried not to think of that. He turned the sheets round, looked again. He concentrated on quality and composition. His work that day had been so confused that there were no more than a handful of shots that met technical requirements.

The pictures sold across the world. The one of the soldier made the cover of a magazine, staring out from the news-stands. He was out around the city the day that it was published. He saw the soldier staring out at the crowds who passed at the ferry pier, saw him rolled in a businessman's hands. He saw him put down flat against a table in a bar and still he knew what was in those eyes. So he fled a second time. He didn't call it flight, but only moving on. He told himself that he would pack up his camera and his few things and move on and learn to take different kinds of pictures, somewhere where there were different pictures to be taken. When the cheque came through it was enough to get away and set himself up in Japan.

2
Tokyo

*I*n Tokyo the eyes are active. They see what is before them. People in Tokyo don't look into themselves but out, and they don't look into you either. That's how it seems in his pictures. That's what he had gone there for. He had gone to photograph Tokyo, capital city of dawning economic miracle. His photographs were intended to be modern, an exploration of modern Japan, of the transitional present. He would photograph Tokyo's streets and Tokyo's new buildings and Tokyo's old buildings and Tokyo's people. What people would do in his pictures, they would do for material reasons, because that was how he wanted to show the nature of this city, and the modern material world into which he wanted to show it was moving. When he photographs people walking through this city, he has all of them look like they are going somewhere, each one of them going somewhere, from one fixed point to another. They walk. They stop at pedestrian lights, at wide junctions where the broad white lines form a square and cross diagonally between. When the lights change, each figure or pair or group of figures takes its particular direction across the road or across the centre of the junction, and he photographs the figures from the slightest downwards

21

angle so that they show as a pattern against the graphic floor of stripes. Sometimes the sun is shining and their shadows fall onto the stripes. Or if it is raining they hold umbrellas above their heads and the stripes become less significant.

They look at things. At their feet on the grey street on which they walk. At the traffic passing. At things in shop windows. At the dishes of plastic food displayed in the windows of restaurants. He photographs them looking, and he photographs the windows, the writing which he cannot read, the plastic food which makes it possible for a foreigner who cannot read a menu to make his choice. Then he looks up and photographs the billboards and the neon, the wires, the ugly ramshackle skyline, the impassive sky. All that is in his pictures when he first comes to Tokyo seems material, except the sky.

He had not expected the cold. Up until now Asia had been only heat to him. He must have known that Japan could be cold. He must at some time have seen pictures of Japan in the snow, photos, prints, Hiroshiges with flakes of snow falling, but the cold of Tokyo at the end of February caught him by surprise. Whatever snow there had been was long past. This was like the familiar chill of a day in English spring, though the air was drier, without the damp grey ache to it that came so often in March at home.

He had to buy warm clothes the morning after he arrived. He asked in the hotel where to shop and they sent him to a department store in Ginza, so that was the first place that he went to. There were pretty girls in uniforms and white gloves greeting customers at the door, and others like dolls in the lifts, but since he could not understand what they said or read the signs, he had to go up the escalators floor by floor to find what he wanted, the floors arranged much as in any department store – cosmetics, women's formal clothes, women's casual clothes, men's clothes, household goods – and there he bought new clothes in which he felt unlike himself. Then he walked away with his bags along the streets, and had a neat Japanese haircut at a barber's that he knew by the red barleysugar-striped pole outside. There were things here in Tokyo that you recognised, others that you didn't, and what interested him, what he would have to try to take pictures of, was the gap between them, he thought, as he sat in the plush red chair, of a type that was familiar from such places everywhere, and watched in the mirror as the barber behind him took up the scissors, and didn't know how to tell him what sort of cut he wanted.

When he came back to his hotel room at the end of the day he stood before the bathroom mirror, and put his hand through the Japanese haircut, and looked at himself. He took out his camera and focused it, held it beside himself and took a picture to record his arrival. He thought he looked blank in the mirror, like no one really, just a Westerner in Tokyo, neither recognisably American nor European, just a nondescript, slightly built young Caucasian male with new clothes and too-short brown hair holding a camera beside his head. But that was the way of so many self-portraits, he thought, that they were blank, unless the artist made an effort, put on a hat, cut off an ear and put a bandage round his head. There was a leather jacket that he had bought. It was the one extravagance of his shopping expedition, affordable because he was still flush with the payment from the magazine. He had taken it off when he had come into the heated room. He put it on again, and ruffled his hair some more and took his self-portrait again wearing the jacket. This was how he would appear to others, as someone strong, individual, whole. Then he put down the camera and looked closely at his reflection in the mirror. He looked into his own eyes, and that was all they were, eyes, grey eyes, looking at themselves, physical things, organs of sight. Cold eyes, they seemed to him, without spirit, material like everything else.

He took the jacket off again. He put on his new sweater over his new shirt, and then the jacket, and wrapped a scarf around his neck, this a rough-woven strip of green raw silk that he had bought on his travels, and went out in Roppongi. It was dark by now. This was a night-life district so everywhere he looked there were bars. He should have gone into one straight away, chosen the first that he saw. Failing to do that, he failed in the end to go into any at all. He walked past one after the other, looking at their signs. He walked until he was past them, all the garish lights behind him. He found side streets that were strangely quiet and small-scale, as if they had forgotten that they were in the centre of a city. He walked on, this way and that through the sleeping domestic streets, hungry by now and longing for a drink, but the bars and restaurants were gone. He was lucky to find a taxi. The seats had lacy covers and the driver wore white gloves like the girls in the department store and drove very smoothly. He had asked to go to the hotel as it was the only place with a name that he knew. He had taken so many twists and turns on his walk that he was surprised that it was so short a distance back along the main avenue. He ate some noodles then from a stall on a street corner, as he might have in South-East Asia only there the night would have been hot, and finally had a beer in the hotel bar. He dreamt that night that he was again in the village in Vietnam. He had had the dream a number of times before, but it had seemed to be fading. This time again it was vivid. There were colours to it: orange dust, and green, and red; red against black, black water, orange soil, stained with red. When he woke in the morning he believed for an instant that he had carried a gun instead of a camera.

All of that next day, he walked. He took pictures on the streets. He walked a long way from his hotel and went into a station somewhere and found himself on the Yamanote Line, which was an easy one for foreigners because it ran in a circle around the city. Even in the station he took pictures, of people waiting on his platform, then of people on the opposite platform lined up for the trains. As long as he stayed in Tokyo he would keep taking these pictures. There was something in them that drew him, the patterns the waiting figures made, the variety of them massed above the orderly horizontal of the railway line, the way particular individuals would stand out, in their dress or by what they were carrying or by their movement, the pragmatic look of people who were waiting, the waiting moments which were blanks, shared interstices in the individual action of each person's day. The green carriages of the Yamanote ran above ground so there was daylight on the stations. When he took pictures in the moving train there was a moving skyline behind the passengers' heads. He turned and took pictures through the thick glass of the window behind him. There were tall buildings within the circle of the Yamanote but outside of it the roofs mostly stretched low and interminably to the horizon. Later in his time in Tokyo when the sky was clear and the pollution was low he would photograph the conical snowcap on Fuji from one of those overground stations. He would not have believed it if he had been told that then, that the mountain could be seen from the city, because the city seemed so vast, complete in itself. He got off at Shinjuku. He went downstairs to find an exit and found that the station itself was another layer of city, a labyrinth underground. When at last he had found his way out, he stopped taking pictures and only walked. He walked on and filled his eyes with pictures. But it wasn't enough. There are images that stay like stains on the memory. However you rub at them, however many other images you gather to replace them with, they don't go. He walked on, following the crowd beneath the towering neon signs. He let himself merge into the crowd, carried along in its current. Though he was short for a man in England he was an ordinary height for a Japanese. He had the Japanese clothes. He had the notion that if he gave himself up to the crowd entirely, identity and memories might wash away.

The less he held to himself, the more he gave to the crowd, he thought, the more he would be a part of the place, understanding it in its present. The less he would have the past with him, the immediate past or any other past besides. That was what he had told himself he had come travelling for, to throw that ballast overboard – the past, that weighed him down. He had told no one where he was. He stood in the crowd at a crossing, waiting for the light to change, seeing the walk-light come up, hearing the bird-song that told the blind to walk, moving when the others moved, across the white lines in a wave. Before going to other places, until now, he had always sent home a *poste restante* address – except for Vietnam. Vietnam would have worried his mother, so he had not told her about Vietnam until afterwards. He might not have told her at all if it had not been for the pictures he sold, and the knowledge that she might come to see them and see his name beneath them. There had been *postes restantes* in Singapore, Jakarta, Denpasar, Bangkok, and then at last in Hong Kong, the best of them airy central post offices with fans suspended from high ceilings where he had queued behind a counter and given his name, received fat airmail envelopes with blue writing on them, numbered and folded pages in response to the brief notes he had written on postcards or on prepaid forms. Jonathan Ashe, *poste restante*: the simplest address. Now there was not even that.

Here he would have no name and no one would know him. He could walk a day through seething streets and see no one eye to eye. He went into a shop. The door slid open automatically, he did not have to touch it, and the shop assistant bowed, just so much that their eyes did not meet. There were greetings they spoke in the shops and in the restaurants, the same words everywhere, *irrashaimasae...*, when he entered and when he left. He did not know what the words meant. He went to a restaurant, and the door slid open untouched, and the words were the same. If they had not said those words at him then he might have had the feeling that he did not exist.

After all, it was being seen that made a person real. He had the sense, when he took pictures and the pictures were developed, that by seeing things and photographing them he was bringing them into existence, fixing some part of their nature that only he had seen. He went back to his hotel room, one small room of so many down a silently carpeted corridor. There again he took a picture of himself. He set the camera up on the table, self-timed a portrait of himself in jeans and grey T-shirt seated on the ruckled sheet with piled white pillows and the bare wall behind him. He took pictures of the room with his few things spread about in the attempt to inhabit it: his jacket on a hanger hung outside not within the wardrobe door, spread papers and camera case on the table. He had bought the English-language newspaper for the ads in it. He could not afford the hotel for long. He laid the paper out on the bed and looked them through.

The apartment he found was out of the centre of the city, down a suburban line that he had not yet travelled. He made his way there according to the directions he was given, turning away from the brash little streets of the entertainment district around the station and going down through a park. Two rooms to sublet from a Canadian Buddhist called Laura while she went to follow a guru in India.

There's a good energy here, Laura said. She spoke so earnestly he had to believe her. There was light. Light, she said, was so important to the Japanese. The two upstairs rooms faced south, each one six mats in floor area, and the value of the rental was based on the aspect and the mat size.

Laura was a pale girl with long blonde hair. She pushed back the windows to show him the view, neat little gardens of evergreens and the backs of houses all irregularly arranged so that no single one seemed to face onto or over-look another. She waved a pale hand at them. Privacy also, she said, was important to the Japanese. Each house had its small unique space, as each person did. She hoped that he wouldn't make much noise? They were careful about noise here. If a person played the saxophone for example, then he might take it and practise in the park. There was someone who did that, who you saw every day at the same time, playing beneath a tree. He didn't play the sax, did he?

Oh, I'm very quiet, Jonathan said.

The girl pushed back the paper doors on the cupboards and showed him where the bedding was kept. Put it down each night and take it up in the morning. Then these rooms seem quite big enough. In the West we have to have our houses so big because we have too many things, don't you think? The Japanese understand how to live without things, with only light and space.

Yes, he said, though he had been seeing the Japanese quite otherwise, but he loved the idea of this apartment. There was a tiny kitchen with two gas rings to cook from and a small window looking onto the narrow residential street, and an even smaller bathroom to bathe in Japanese-style, where he would squat to wash first and then take a very hot dip in the deep plastic bath.

You fill it cold and put it on for thirty minutes to heat the water, she told him. But careful, don't boil the bathtub.

I'd like to take the flat, he said. When do you come back from India?

She pushed some vague blonde hair back behind her ear. I'm not sure, she said. It's hard to keep track once you get to the ashram. Let's say three months for now. Is that OK, three months? Or maybe six? That would take us through till September, September's beautiful here. But I'll send you a card before then. I'll send you a card and say how it's going.

Then she took him to meet the landlady who lived downstairs, a tiny old woman in a grey kimono. Laura went into the hallway and spoke to her in Japanese while he hovered at the threshold unsure whether to take off his shoes and enter.

Mrs Ozawa says that's fine.

And Mrs Ozawa spoke directly to him and bowed to him, low, and he bowed too. He was glad that he was still standing below the threshold or he would have felt impolitely tall.

One other thing, Laura said, before you go. They went back up the stairs and she gave him the keys and showed where the lock was tricky, and then pointed out the plant that grew in a large pot right beside the entrance. There's a hornets' nest. Look. She tapped the dry case of the nest which was grey and papery, just a few inches long, suspended from the stem of the plant. Or at least, there was last year. If they come back you won't kill them, will you?

Postcard

I'm in Tokyo now. I'm going to settle here for a while. I've got a flat here, in a quiet district, the sort of place you'd like. It's near the park and it's an old house, and there are bamboos and clipped bushes in the gardens, and the streets are so small that they have toy fire engines as full-size ones couldn't get through if one of the houses caught fire. My landlady is very small and very old. It's all very neat, and the rubbish is collected in a tiny rubbish cart three times a week. The walk from the underground station goes through a park and there's a temple in the park and the cherry blossom's out.

The postcard showed a detail of a shrine, an edge of dark cedar wall and a curve of shingle roof with cherry blossom about it. The gardens were the bit of Japan his mother would like. He wrote the card and then it sat on the low table in the living room for days, until he added a postscript.

This is my address: 5-2-18 Inokashira. I know it looks odd. It's really a kind of map reference as the streets don't seem to have names.

It was a postcard, not a letter. It was so much easier to write a postcard and say nothing. And he had written almost as if he was a child or as if he was writing to a child, as if their relationship was stuck so far back. His mother would take it in her hand and like the picture because she always liked flowers, and then she would read what he had said and think her own thoughts about the place, whatever they might be, but she would have no idea, no understanding at all, of why he was there. Jonathan's in Japan now, she would say to his brother when his brother came in, her voice soft in the room, and there would be a pause before Richard replied. Would there be an edge in her voice or would it be no more than a statement of fact? Look, the card's there on the table. A clear, musical voice she had, an indoors voice. Richard would have been out on the tractor all day, perhaps – if it had not rained, if the weather was kind and the land fit for drilling – out on the tractor also in his own thoughts, and talk of Japan would take him by surprise. Japan, or rather the Japanese, had been their father's domain. Had enough time passed now, or would the word bring into this brief pause the memory of their father?

He put the postcard up on the shelf by the door where he kept the keys so that he could take it to post next time he went out. Yet when he did go out he walked by it. And he walked by it again and again. Each time he came in or went out he saw it, the pink froth of cherry blossom about the dark curve of the shrine roof. He could have written more with each day that passed. He could have told them how very different the place was from whatever they might imagine, how different the Japanese were. He was paying his way by teaching them

33

English. Every Japanese, it seemed, wanted to learn English, and any wandering English speaker could find work easily enough. He had signed up with a language school, the one Laura had worked for, taken on Laura's private students as well as her flat while she was gone. There was a girl he taught, one of Laura's students, who had a photograph of a different boyfriend in the same picture frame on her coffee table each of the three times he had gone to her house to teach; he hadn't been there often enough yet to see if the photos and the boyfriends were rotated. And there was a microsurgeon, evidently very skilled, who wanted to learn English conversation before he took up a senior post in a hospital in Kentucky. He had absolutely no small talk but an extensive technical vocabulary, and when he ran out of other words he would show gory slides of operations he had performed, explain in detail the reattachment of lost fingers and hands and limbs.

What does he want to go there for? Richard would have said.

These were not the people his father had fought. The microsurgeon said that orientals had greater dexterity in surgery because they used chopsticks from an early age. Their fingers developed exceptional precision and strength. And he looked at the man's hands and saw that they were indeed fine and delicate.

Richard was four years older, his big brother; always his big brother not only by his age but by his build and his size, and his place in the world. What are you going anywhere for? he might have said. Richard had gone away only as far as agricultural college, and then done the right thing, come back home to his mother and taken the farm in hand. He had told Richard about his plan for the trip to Asia before he had told his mother. Richard had thought he was off on the hippy trail.

Going to be a hippy, are you, then?

No, a photographer. He did not say that aloud at the time, but only to himself. Richard would not have understood the weight each of those four syllables had for him, the ambition. Richard would have laughed, as he had always laughed at his dreams. Richard's dream, if he had one, was in the soil at his feet.

He wrote only to his mother, not to Richard, but what he wrote he expected that Richard would read as well. Look, there's Jonathan's card. I'm sure it's for you too. As she or someone will surely have said, sometime before, Look, Jonathan's had some pictures published in a magazine. What Richard thought when he saw those pictures, he couldn't say. At least he would not have laughed. Would Richard have been impressed, that he had actually done something with his camera, had his name beneath the pictures, earned some money, or would they have stirred up the past, as his coming to Japan must have stirred up the past, as if all the things that he was doing so far away yet disturbed the past already made at home? You saw, Richard said once. Richard had accused him of seeing, and now he had made it his profession to see.

He pushed back the paper screens from the window, and the glass ones behind them, knelt on the floor where he could rest his elbows on the sill, took pictures of his view. He took the same pictures repeatedly, as if to make a study of his surroundings through all of the times of the day, the differing lights and shadows. Before he will leave this apartment, he will have taken hundreds of the same shots.

The shots of the gardens are full of oblique angles, form dictating their composition as within the gardens themselves, where the positioning of trees and shrubs is careful and their shapes are controlled, foliage and style of growth more important to the gardener than flowers. Only rarely are there people to be seen in these gardens, but there is always the notion of people within the houses behind them, screened from view, here and there some bedding hung out from a window or balcony to air, a rectangle of bright artificial colour above the overall deep green of the plants below. From the small window in the kitchen there are other shots, these also angled but that is of necessity, because of the awkwardness of the position of the window. These shots show the rails of the external metal staircase leading to his door, the big pot with the hibiscus in it – it is possible to gauge the month when the photograph is taken by the leaves, which are absent in the first shots because the hibiscus comes into leaf so late, but fresh green and obscuring in others that follow. Then beyond the stair and the pot there is a narrow perspective down the street, and here there are figures, single or paired but rarely more than that: Mrs Ozawa or some other elderly neighbour walking hunched over a stick, a mother with a child in a buggy, older children walking to or from school with leather satchels on their backs. Generally the pictures show women because this is a purely residential district inhabited in the hours of daylight almost entirely by women and children and very old men.

Often when he had been into the central parts of the city he stopped in the entertainment district by the station on his way home. Even after the late trains, there were bars that stayed open when everything else was closing, people who hung about as the streets darkened and the lights went out. There was a bar that he found, that he got to like. He had found it by chance, Ken's Bar, the sign hand-printed in roman letters pointing up a flight of stairs. The walls of the bar were bare planed wood and the cramped space smelled of beer and pungent Japanese cigarettes, and a little of the wood itself. There were two places he particularly liked to sit, one at a table by the first-floor window from which he could look down on the narrow street, the last lit lanterns and stray salarymen, the other on a stool by the bar. The barman – Ken, he guessed it was, almost always the same barman and he appeared to own the place – had a steady presence. If you sat up there you sat close to him, and a nodding relationship was easy but there was no require-ment for more. After a few visits he bought his own bottle of whisky to keep behind the bar. He had to spell out his name for Ken to write on the label. It looked strange to him when the bottle went up beside the others on the shelf, the one English name alongside all the names in Japanese.

Could you write my name in Japanese instead?

You want Japanese writing? Not *kanji*. *Katakana* I can do.

It was late at night and there were only a couple of other customers in the place, and Ken had nothing better to do than watch and wipe the counter clean. He took the bottle down again, and Jonathan said his name again, pronouncing each syllable precisely and adding a hint of a final vowel to the last consonant, *jo-na-tha-nu*, and Ken wrote out a new label in the phonetic script the Japanese use for foreign words.

That's better.

But he kept the bottle down beside him and topped up his drink, added water from the jug on the counter.

Do you get other gaijin here? Gaijin was the word Japanese used for foreigners, and it was used so pervasively that every gaijin learned it within days of arrival.

One American came, last week. You American?

British.

From London?

From Norfolk. That's in the east. A long way from London.

What you do in Tokyo?

I take pictures.

Many pictures to take in Tokyo.

His English wouldn't carry the conversation much further. Jonathan took up the bottle again and made the whisky darker in his glass.

39

He was in Tokyo. He was in a bar in Tokyo. A man had asked him where he came from and the thought had pulled at him, pulled him down inside himself where there were other thoughts that he did not want to think. And he had drunk too much whisky.

Much later he asked, When do you close?

Morning.

So he stayed until morning, or at least until dawn. Some new customers came in and made vague company, and he stayed there slowly drinking, and his Japanese seemed to improve with the drink, and he didn't think too much, and time passed more easily the more of it passed and he did not see it go. When he stumbled down the stairs at last it was beginning to get light. The street cleaners were out in front of the station, working round a few slumped figures on benches. He walked by them with his camera in the bag on his shoulder. He walked into the park. He felt that he was past sleeping. If he did not sleep then he would not have to dream. There was a path that led through the park, past a police box and over a bridge across a little lake, directly towards the street where he lived. He didn't go right through but instead turned away along the edge of the lake. There was a fine mist just over the water, and the water was opaque and the carp in it were hidden, save for when one broke the surface and set a ripple going. He should have taken pictures but he didn't remove the camera from its bag. He walked on through trees as if he had left the city altogether, and at last he came to another gate, and went

40

out into little streets where he got lost, and it was a long time before he found his way home.

He should have taken pictures. Photographers like to take pictures in the early morning, when the light is soft and things are only just becoming themselves. The early morning is when discoveries are made, things seen that could not be seen in the night and that would not be allowed to be exposed under the bright light of day. When reality is either questionable or most itself. When a farmer who has not slept all night goes out where the fog hangs over the flat land, and there's a shot in the woods and the pigeons are shaken suddenly into flight. And a boy who is awake early goes out and walks along the edge of the plough and into the trees to see. And the plough falls away into rice fields, and the fields are flooded and there are green shoots in the water, and the path is narrow and the village is burning, and there is smoke or perhaps it is mist and there is crimson in the mist, and first it is flame but then it is blood, on the ground, such a pooling of blood.

Richard

Where were you?
        When?
This morning. I looked in your room. Where were you?
Nowhere.

Richard was blocking his way. They were in the corridor at the foot of the stairs. Ahead of him, beyond Richard's body, it led to the back door and the kitchen. Behind was upstairs, and the hall and the bolted front door and the sitting room, and his father's study, and he didn't want to go that way.

You went out. Your boots are muddy. I saw, the mud's wet.

I didn't go anywhere.

Richard grabbed him, grabbed his arm and twisted him round and bent his arm and held it in a half nelson, high up the centre of his back, pressing it higher.

The corridor was dark and he could see his boots at the end of it, in the light that came in through the narrow pane of glass above the back door, his boots lined up with the others where he had taken them off and put them so

neatly side by side when he had come in, when he had crept upstairs in his socks and thought that no one would know, when already he wasn't sure what he had seen, and thought that if he went back to bed and got up again then it would be gone like a dream as if it hadn't happened at all.

Let go. The pain shot through his arm. He didn't know if some of him was actually breaking.

Then their mother came out from the kitchen and Richard dropped his arm in a flash. She didn't notice anything because there was someone at the back door. It was Billy Eastmond there, and some other men, and one of them was a policeman. He felt strong now that the pain had gone.

I was just having an adventure. You don't have adventures. I'm going to have more adventures than you ever will.

3
Kumiko

*T*he photographs travel the city. At Shinjuku station people pass through smooth conduits, channelled between one action and the next. Light shines equally off the hard surfaces of walls and floor and ceiling, and the moving people make soft-edged shadows where they go. In Kanda, in the business district, two salarymen bow to one other in the street. He photographs them from the side so that they appear like mirror reflections of themselves, in dress and position and in the identical briefcases they carry, and the image is repeated but broken and jumbled amongst all the other reflections in the glass of the building behind them. In Akihabara, he photographs whole streets of electrical and camera stores, rising floor upon floor, graphic upon graphic, window displays packed with televisions and cameras, aisles within stacked to the ceiling with hi-fis and speakers, streams of dark-haired men milling beneath. He photographs from behind the heads of men who crowd to inspect the newest systems, the black domes of heads before the circling black disc on a wall-mounted record deck, which seems to mesmerise when placed at eye level, playing vertically before them, or again from behind, a row of black heads wearing headphones to listen to

47

quality of sound. He has taken those photographs and walked on elsewhere. A young couple walk in front of him in the street, the young man's hand around the young woman's waist, and the picture he takes is of his hand, resting with the thumb to the girl's waist, the lowest finger to the curve of her hip, his arm bare save for a metal watch strap on his wrist – his right wrist, indicating that he is most likely a left-handed man, and this is all that there is to distinguish him. In Shibuya, he photographs a vast billboard carrying an advertisement for Dior perfume. A teenage girl walks beneath the three-quarter profile of a beautiful and sophisticated Caucasian woman – Caucasian, not Japanese, because the ideal above this girl will be Western, not Japanese – whose dangling diamond earring is the same length as the girl. In this image as in the others his regard is impersonal, the figures similarly impersonal, reduced at times to no more than forms. A girl has the same value as an earring. Perhaps they cannot be otherwise because he is so foreign here. He sees this when he looks over the photographs so much later, he sees what he was doing. Or, it was what Tokyo was doing to him. There were so many of them, so many Japanese, the population of this city so numerous and so homogeneous, so Japanese. He thought that he looked for individuals but he could apprehend these people only in the mass. It made him all the more solitary. This is what the pictures show: not so much the world about him but his own solitariness behind the lens.

Kumiko worked at the language school. He saw her on the first day he went there, and he saw her after that whenever he went in. He had known her for some time before he dared to take her picture.

She had a wide smile and her skin was dark and a little coarse, her attractiveness like that of pottery, not porcelain. She wore brightly coloured clothes, short skirts, coloured tights, but more often jeans and skimpy tops and a short black jacket. He saw all that. He saw, and saw her intently, but spoke to her no more than the job required. Hi. *Ohayu.* How do I get to this student's house? If the directions were difficult she might take up the telephone and talk to the student in Japanese, and draw him a map. She drew deftly, a map from some subway exit, turn left at the first lights, over the pedestrian bridge, right or left at the bakery or the coffee shop or the noodle bar, you'll find the building two blocks down on the left. He watched her small hands and then her face as she drew, with her eyes turned down to the paper. She looked up and smiled again before he had taken his look away. He took the paper when her hands had left it and folded it safe into his wallet, and found that he too was smiling as he went out. He waited for the lift. The language school was just three rooms on a fourth floor with a big sign downstairs and a small one inside the lift. By the time the lift doors opened he was closed in himself again. He went down and out again into the crowds.

One day he went to a new student, a salaryman in his forties by the look of him, wearing a grey suit and opening to him the scuffed white door of a small and nondescript flat some place out towards Yokohama. It had been a long way to go for a single hour's conversation class. The man lived

49

alone and the flat was stuffy. He could see into the narrow
kitchen that was like his own with a double gas ring and
washing-up piled in the sink. The man made coffee, then
they sat across a table and made stilted conversation and
added to the pile of white cigarette ends in the ashtray – long
cigarette ends since the Japanese never seemed to smoke
a cigarette right down but lit another, as if by doing that they
would save themselves from cancer. The man looked all a
bit rumpled, like a salaryman not in the afternoon but after
a night out. A salaryman should have been in his office at
that time of day, but Jonathan didn't ask what he was doing
at home. He had made it a habit in these encounters not
to ask anything personal. He had found that it was easier,
with male students in particular, to read a passage about
some neutral subject, hobbies or sport, and set the conversation off that way. This man's English was quite good.
He said that he liked to hike and to go fishing, and sometimes he played golf. More often, he said, he just went to
the driving range. He spoke expressionlessly as if he was
only building sentences and their meaning was irrelevant,
so that Jonathan was unsure whether these were actually his
hobbies or whether they simply happened to be the words
that came to his mind. Sometimes I go to the driving range,
he said. It is only a short range, seventy-five yards, but it is
local and it is inexpensive. I practise my drive all afternoon.
His grammar was good but his vocabulary was limited.
When Jonathan attempted to move him into other subject
areas he had trouble. Frequently he paused to find a word.
He was very precise and would not ask for help or use any

alternative, any roundabout expression, but leaf through a big Japanese dictionary, and the conversation would freeze until he had tapped another Mild Seven out from the packet and lit it, and found exactly the word that he wanted, yet still Jonathan was not convinced that its meaning mattered.

Your English is good, Jonathan said as he left. What you need to do is more reading, to increase your vocabulary. Then you would speak it really well.

The man stood with his hand on the door, close because the hallway was small. You are the first person I have spoken with in six weeks, he said. Jonathan thought he was saying that it was the first time he had spoken English, but then he saw that the man did indeed mean spoken, that this was the first conversation of any kind that he had had in all that time.

They stood in the tiny hallway, very close.

I lost my job, six weeks ago. I cannot tell that to anyone. The man's voice and eyes were flat, without expression.

But you must talk to someone. How about your family?

My family is in Chiba.

Why don't you go and see them?

I cannot tell them.

Go and see them, tell them something else for now.

He opened the door and Jonathan went out, then turned to shake his hand. He felt the responsibility of it, of shaking this man's hand.

See you next week then.

He went the next week, all the way out on the Yokohama Line, using the map once more as the route was complicated and all the streets looked much the same. Right by the playground, left at the bakery, count the blocks. He got to the building, pressed the button by the door, waited. No one answered. He went across the street and looked up to the windows of the flat on the second floor but they were closed and there was no light or life to be seen. There was a little wall there before a parking space and he sat down on it to wait. He must have waited out the full length of the lesson on that little wall opposite the house, occasionally going across and pressing again on the bell.

He went back to the language school, not home, though it was a long journey so he got there only just before it closed. Kumiko was on her way out. That new student you sent me to, Mr Miyazaki. He wasn't there.

Maybe he forgot.

I don't think so. Can you phone him?

So she went back in to the reception desk and took up the phone and while it rang he told her about Mr Miyazaki.

That's terrible, she said. He must be so lonely. After a long time she put down the phone.

Maybe he did what you said and went to Chiba.

I don't think so.

Then to the driving range. He had told her about the golf as well.

Could you try him again later? When do those places close?

I don't know. I think they stay open late.

Beneath their words the image flashed of lonely Mr Miyazaki in leisure clothes, with the iron carefully held in his two hands, positioning, swinging, driving, through the afternoon and into the night, floodlit in the great green cage of the driving range. He saw it, and he thought that she saw it too.

Before she locked up she wrote down the telephone number and put it into her bag. They got into the lift together. She made the steel space warm with her presence.

Where are you going now? he said.

They went to a tempura restaurant close by the language school. To have travelled somewhere else would have made it too much of a date. It was a traditional place with bamboo outside and dark wooden booths within, and almost empty. When she took off her black jacket she was the brightest thing there.

It's a lunchtime place but I came here once before with my boss when we had to work late.

It's fine, he said. It's nice.

You like to drink sake?

Yes.

It was nice to have her order the food and see it put before them, better than he could have selected for himself. To see her hands pour the warm sake from pottery flask to small pottery cup and to feel the glow of it when he drank.

He told her that he had been travelling. He told her about Indonesia, how there had been ferries from island to island, jungle, volcanoes, beaches. Then about Thailand, Hong

Kong. Not Vietnam. Only the light things. He could not reconcile the weight in him with the lightness of his contacts here, the sense that he was floating in this alien city, that the city was a floating world, all its crowds and lights and colours. Even Mr Miyazaki was floating, like a lone man on a raft out in the ocean. The girl's face drew him, her hands on the sake cup, as if she alone was rooted in the earth.

She asked about his home. In that moment it seemed unimportant. Only the present moment mattered.

Where do you come from? London?

No, not London. Always they asked him that. From the countryside. My family has a farm.

That happy smile, the warmth of her. What sort of animals do you have?

No animals. It's all arable. This he must explain as she does not know the word. We grow things. Wheat, potatoes, things like that. It's very different kind of country from here. Flat, with big skies. There are no mountains like in Japan, no volcanoes, no earthquakes. He looked into her eyes and wanted to say more, something about the weight and flatness of the land he came from, that seemed something he wanted to tell her about himself, about the frozen weight of its geological past that was so different from all that she knew. He could not say that to this girl. He did not know why he suddenly wanted to say that. He said only that he meant to take some trips into the countryside, that he had not so much as gone yet to Hakone, or Fuji.

And you must go to the coast, she said. Izu, maybe. I know a place in Izu.

Where's that?

On the coast, like I said. And of course you have to go to Kyoto. And there's Nikko, that's an easy day trip, but it's most beautiful in the winter, in the snow.

Someone told me I should go to Kamakura.

My grandfather lives in Kamakura, she said. The temple there is famous for its flowers.

What kind of flowers?

Hydrangeas.

He wasn't sure he much liked hydrangeas but he didn't say so.

I'll take you there, she said.

They travelled back together as far as Shinjuku where each of them took a different line. They said goodbye there, on her platform, then he went to find his own. He saw her enter her train, small and jaunty, and the doors closing behind her. He turned in the other direction and then he got lost. Every gaijin gets lost sometimes in Tokyo, he told himself. Perhaps even the Japanese were sometimes lost. He wished that the girl was still with him. Perhaps it was the loss of her presence that made him lost now. He thought that he had learned his way round Shinjuku. He went there every day and yet he had never been to that particular plat-form before and now none of the tunnels he entered looked familiar to him. He saw signs for every train line but his own, so many different train lines, so many exits, innumer-able connecting tunnels between them, and people walking as they always did underground, not strolling but with their directions fixed, even in the evening when there should be no urgency any more, when they must have had a meal or a drink, though it was early still and there were not the drunks about yet, when they should be relaxed or just slow and tired, going home. He came to an exit and went up, for air if for nothing else, though perhaps he thought also that it might be easier to orient himself above ground. He climbed the steps into the night and into the equally incomprehensible sprawl of the streets, but here at least there were colours and traffic, distinct sights and sounds, strips of sound that he walked through and escaped, passing from one sound to another, and there were people, and people were different above ground, talking, laughing, stumbling, milling about, not closed like the automata underground, and high above the lights, above the neon signs and all the lit floors of the buildings, there must be a black sky. He walked on, knowing that he could not become more lost. After a while he came to an open area, and there was another entrance to the station, and at the top of the steps two tall gaijin men. He could see that they were American. There was something about them that made it obvious, some openness, stance, confidence of manner. These two wore suits and were almost militarily clean-cut, standing smartly as soldiers are supposed to stand but more smartly than the soldiers that he had known. Mormon missionaries; there were lots of them in Tokyo. They were always in pairs, and they spoke Japanese, and Japanese girls thought them handsome. He asked how to get to his line and they told him the way.

He didn't have any classes that took him into the school until the following week. She was there at the desk wearing a yellow dress.

I called Mr Miyazaki.

Does he want me this week?

He didn't answer. I called that night when I got home, and then in the morning here in the office. I call him every morning but there's no reply.

Again, there was Mr Miyazaki between them. But she looked very pretty in the dress.

He didn't pay, she said.

If he had no job then probably he had no money.

Then he can't pay his rent either.

So he will have gone. Maybe he's just gone.

If he has no job, he thought, if a salaryman has no salary, what is he then?

At the weekend he had finally written a letter home. The postcard on the shelf was too old by now, the cherry blossom long fallen. The card itself looked worn from lying around so long. So he had sat down on a cushion on the floor at the low table before the window, the window open to the May air and the quiet of the gardens, and written to his mother. It was the thought of Miyazaki that had made him write. The letter was the longest he had written since he had gone away. He had told his mother again about where he lived, and Mrs Ozawa downstairs, how he was taking pictures and teaching English, but he wrote more this time. He told her the good things about Japan, that there was a courtesy to everything, and that though the city was ugly on the surface people took the old aesthetic very seriously, and every now and then you came upon a piece of the old aesthetic and it was beautiful. There were shops in Ginza where they sold beautiful fruits, melons that were prized for the perfection of the patterns on their skin, and these were sold as gifts for twenty times their value as fruits, and were put into cushioned boxes and carefully wrapped to be taken away. He had written that, and then he had read it over and wondered why he had chosen to write about the melons. He had read over the whole letter, and saw that it was written from a great distance, the distance between Japan and England, but also the distance between his words and himself. He had thought that he should begin again and write something that closed the distance, but he had sealed the envelope and decided to send it anyway.

I wrote a letter, he said to the girl. I need a stamp. Can I scrounge one off you?

For England? I don't think we have any but I'll see.

There was no one else in the office. He was waiting for a group of students to come and then he would give a lesson in the classroom there.

He had told his mother about the flowers as well. People go at particular seasons, he told her, to view the flowers.

When do the hydrangeas come out?

Not for a while.

Can we go somewhere before then?

I'm free on Saturday. What are you doing on Saturday?

I take pictures, he had told the girl. I'd like to see them, she said. But there were so many rolls of film now, stacked on the shelves in the door of his fridge, stored in the cool until he got round to having them processed. When he went out, he took more. When a film was finished, he rewound it and removed it and put it into his bag, and reloaded the camera, and when he thought about it he took whatever rolls of film there were out from his bag and put them away in the fridge, yellow rolls into their black canisters put away in the whiteness beside the milk and the orange juice, that a picture in itself. Then he closed the door and left them in the dark. Will you show them to me? she said. If he was to do that then he would have first to see what was good enough to show, print what might make sense to another person's eyes. You can't see any yet, I have to get them printed first. For himself, he thought, it did not matter now. Perhaps it was only the seeing that mattered right now, the way he saw through the camera, the way that the camera taught him to see. Don't you have any at all? I sent a lot home, he said, when I was travelling. Some of his tourist shots of the islands, his first impressions of

Asia, he had packaged up and sent home. He still had others, but they were packed away. He wasn't sure what he had and what he didn't have, what was and what was not developed. There was some stuff from Hong Kong, and there were the contacts of Vietnam. There's nothing, he said, just a lot of rolls of film. So she offered to find him a professional lab. Thanks, he said. He could not explain his reluctance even to himself. But there are an awful lot of them, you know. To print them would be to fix them, one instant after another, all the instants of his days here repeated in the sheets frame by frame, moments that he had seen and forgotten beside the moments that he remembered – and none of them important, none mattering in the slightest against what had gone before.

On Saturday will you bring your camera?

Of course. He brought his camera everywhere.

The pictures he would have liked to have shown her were other pictures, quite other things altogether. The things that were permanent, not instants, even when they were gone. He wanted to show her those things so that she would begin to know who he was.

They met at Shinjuku where they had said goodbye the other night. He found his way easily this time so he was there early and saw her come out of her train. She was wearing cropped jeans and white plimsolls, and she had her hair in a ponytail which made her look like a child. They took a long journey then right across the city to the docklands, where he had been only once before. There was a garden there that had originally been the garden to a palace.

He took his first photographs of her standing beneath an arbour of wisteria. She stood very simply with her two hands joined before her, her face more delicate with the hair pulled back and the delicate flowers hanging about it, and the shadows of them on her cheek. He took one of her solemn and one of her smiling. Later he would take that smiling image and blow it up, and smell again the scent of the flowers.

Fire

Now that she had his address, his mother wrote him letters again. The letters told him about the weather and the garden, and had pieces of news in them about what Richard was doing on the farm, or about people in the village to whose names he sometimes couldn't put a face. What touched him most was when one said how the swallows had come back and were nesting again under the eaves. That took him home more than any rational thought. He went out then and bought an airmail form, and sat down in a coffee shop and wrote a brief reply, long enough only to just about fill the inside page of the form.

I saw a strange thing the other day, when I was standing at a bus stop on my way to give a lesson. A house burned down before my eyes. There was smoke rising across the street, and flames suddenly on a rooftop. I had my camera on me, I always have my camera on me, so I crossed the road and went to see. It was down the side street, a little wooden house of a type they have all over the place here, one of the older houses squeezed in now among the newer ones. There was nobody in it. There was just the house, and it seemed to burn down in no time – or most of it had gone before the fire engine came and we few bystanders were waved back to the main road. I don't know if the pictures will be any good. I should have got there a bit sooner, when the flames were clear and before the roof fell in. All there was to photograph by the time I was there was just chaos and smoke, no form to it any more. It made me think of the stubble burning, the pictures I took at home the year before I came away. Do you remember? I took a load of pictures of the stubble being set light to, and the fire moving across the field, and the rats running from it. I suppose that if there were any rats in the house they got away before I reached the scene. (Never seen rats in Japan though, only cockroaches, big ones in my flat. The previous tenant's a Buddhist and wouldn't kill them.)

Anyway, once the firemen got their hoses on it the flames died and the smoke turned heavy and black, and I went back to the bus stop and everyone who had been there before was still waiting – maybe the fire engine had held up the traffic or something – and it seemed as if nothing had happened at all. I was late for the lesson of course. I'm not sure how long I'm going to keep up this English teaching. I waste a lot of time travelling that I don't get paid for. I need to get some photography work but it's hard to make the contacts without speaking the language.

He folded the fine blue paper. How flimsy everything was, how thin his words. How light and without weight.

You chose the words and you chose the significance to attach to them but you could not control the other significances that came to mind even when you did not give them words. You saw the house burn down and you wrote of the stubble burning. You consciously brought up the memory of yourself and Richard setting fire to the stubble after harvest, Richard there with his gun to shoot the running vermin and yourself with the camera, the white smoke rising into the September sky and the whole event controlled so that the fire did not spread, you tried to flick a switch in your memory and you wrote of that, but there was quite another memory vivid in your mind. There were the images of burning and there were the sounds that went with them, the crackle of stubble, the falling-in of the pieces of a house, and behind and above them a roar that was like wind but that was not wind, that was made of the fire and the rush and the screams.

He felt shaken inside, even as he licked the glued edges of the paper to close the letter and hold down the airy words within it. He took a sip of his coffee but it had gone cold. The dainty cake he had ordered was something to look at rather than to eat. He looked about the coffee shop that was a bland imitation of some European cafe with its little white tables and white-painted bentwood chairs and plasterwork like the icing on the cake. The trio of girls at the next table noticed him looking, and lowered their heads now like geisha and giggled behind their hands. Things in this place were so light, hollow, none of them quite real. He thought that he might stay a long time.

He began to get his pictures of Tokyo developed at the lab she found for him. He didn't get them done in any particular order. He hadn't dated or labelled the rolls. He took in a few at a time, when he had the money for it, and got the contact sheets done but had only a handful of images printed. The lab was close to the language school so when he came there he had the envelopes in his hand.

He showed her the first lot of prints and she asked to see the contacts as well. These were not meant for people to see, he said. Most of them were rubbish, images that came before and after and beside whatever it was that would make a photograph.

But won't you let me see them?

OK. They were random, did she not know that? He felt vulnerable showing them, as if he were exposing to her his flawed thoughts.

These are from when I first arrived.

*   *   *

Kumiko held one sheet in her hand and then another, and looked them over. You took a lot, she said, with her big warm smile. Yet he could see that she was not impressed with the pictures he had taken of the city. Their subjects must be things that she took for granted, surfaces and nothing more, and their composition must then seem imperfect, off-centre, unsatisfying. So he showed her what was pretty. He showed her what she wanted to see. He showed her the self that he wanted her to see and put away the rest.

She liked his flowers best. The sheets of flowers she laid down on the table and he gave her a glass so that she could look more closely. He had taken a complete roll of cherry blossom, first whole trees and then frame after frame filled only with flowers, a fine black framework of branches and a luminous mass of petals like spray across them.

Why do you take them in black and white?

To show their form, he said. And because of the way the flowers take the light. See how the light seems almost to come through them.

The cumulative effect in the contact sheets was powerful. She moved with the glass from one image to the next. How do you choose, she asked, which one you will print? He took the glass from her hand. He moved the glass to another frame, stood back to let her see. She bent forward, taking the glass again from his fingers. There were things a photographer looked for, he said, subtle variations between the shots, alterations in shutter setting, contrast, depth of

66

field. She did not have the eye for it, she told him. He was aware of her closeness beside him, her small smooth hand with the glass in it resting beside his on the glossy sheets in the sunlight. He was aware of the delicacy of her hand, the tone and texture of her Japanese skin that was so very different from his own. The fine line of difference ran between their two hands on the table.

You should take more in colour, she said.

I have some in colour. I'll show you another time. I have another series of flowers, of the wisteria at Hama Rikyu, but I don't have them developed yet. I went back, after that day when we went together, and took some more.

They went out together again that evening. In the restaurant it was easy to talk. It was a noisy place and full of action. Then they left and there were just the two of them, and they fell silent. They walked to the subway and he put his arm beneath her jacket to her waist. They kissed in the dark of the street, and again when they parted in the bright light of the station. When they did that, they closed their eyes to make it dark.

He took colour film when they went to Kamakura but the photographs should have been black and white. It was a day for black and white. Only the shiny red of her raincoat justifies his use of colour, seeming to glow against the grey and the wet. From all of that day there is perhaps just one picture of her that is worth keeping, and even that one isn't as good as it might be. The image would not stand alone without what his memory can add to it.

They looked out from the train and saw suburban Tokyo stretching away in the rain, black-tiled roofs and some-times red and blue roofs shining with the wet, the sky a nothingness above them.

It's the rainy season, she said. It will rain like this for weeks. Her face was soft in the smeary light that came through the window of the train.

Kamakura's streets were full of umbrellas. They walked up to the hydrangea temple. The wood of the temple buildings was dark with the wet. They were too early for the flowers. The leaves of the hydrangeas were prolific, green and weighted with moisture, but the flowers had only begun to bud.

You will have to come back and take pictures when they come out. Then there are so many people here, it's like Tokyo station, and everyone taking pictures.

It's fine, he said. It's nice like this. He was happy to see it as it was. There was just a scattering of visitors, and their umbrellas did not so much as reach to the knee of the giant seated Buddha, monumental above them with the rain streaming down the folds of his robes and his head dissolving blackly into the mist. Elsewhere, in the surrounding gardens, there was no one but themselves. They walked up steps and along pathways and found shelter for a while beneath a temple gateway, watching the rain fall beyond the overhanging curve of roof. It was a fine rain but constant.

It doesn't stop, this rain.

I told you, she said, it goes on for weeks.

It must stop sometimes.

OK, sometimes it does. But you'll see, nothing ever gets dry.

She pointed out that one shoulder of his leather jacket was wet where he had held the umbrella over her more than over himself.

Now we shall go and see my grandparents, she said, and they walked downhill and along backstreets. Her grandparents were getting old so she tried to see them often.

My grandfather is losing his memory, she said. I like to get him to talk, to have him say things so that I can remember for him.

What does he talk about?

Oh, the past. How things used to be. You will see, he is an old man. He wears a kimono like old men do and he grows bonsai. You must ask him about his bonsai.

He thought, he could not find his way back if she were not to come with him. They had come through so many small streets and turnings, down and then up and around the back of the hill, and all of the streets looked similar in the rain, the view narrow with the umbrella low over their heads, a view of dripping eaves and wet pavement, and other people with umbrellas, stepping aside, and a woman on a bicycle, wearing a transparent plastic cape and a flowery sou'wester, gliding by.

My grandmother will be lonely when he forgets.

He looked at her face that was different that day with the heavy hair down across it, and a touch of lipstick and the collar of her red raincoat turned up to her chin. Stop there a moment, he said, and he took a picture of her, at that angle, so close to him, but already the look on her face had changed. Japanese girls had a way of showing you the child in them at the same time as the woman, that captivated, that he didn't know how he'd catch in a single picture.

They came to the house and it was an old one built of darkened wood and set back from the road behind a sliding wooden gate, and there were three bonsai trees in glazed pots before the entrance. Later he would understand that they were very good ones but he did not pay them much attention because he had not yet learned the particularities of bonsai. Kumiko called out and her grandmother came to the door as they took off their shoes, the old woman in a dull-green kimono kneeling on the threshold and bowing to him in greeting, all in Japanese, pointing to the rack where he must put his shoes and the slippers that he might take instead, he feeling suddenly ungainly, his feet too large and his socks holed, too foreign and brutish for this delicate setting. He bowed as low as he could, and Kumiko's look suggested that she found his actions comical, and then he went through into the house and bowed to the old man, and the four of them sat on the floor and drank tea from small brown cups about a low table, the three others speaking and himself silent, sipping the sharply flavoured green tea. Even Kumiko looked somehow misplaced, bigger than the old people, too bright and modern, so that you would think they must each time they saw her be surprised to know that she was the child of their child. The old woman had a neatness of movement and a fineness of feature beneath her thin white hair that would always have been there, even when she was young, but the old man seemed to have shrivelled back on his frame, stooped and slow-moving, bony head and hands almost out of scale with the rest of him.

Jonathan looked at him and thought that when he was shown the bonsai, stepping down from the veranda at the back of the house when there was an interval in the rain, nodding as if he understood what the old man said as they passed from one wizened tree to the next. Instead of seeing them for what they were, as plants root-pruned and restrained from the start as they grew, he had a sense of trees that had once been tall but that had reduced with the years, contracted year by year into thick-barked miniatures of themselves. Then they went on past the line of bonsai into the garden, while the women remained indoors talking. The garden too was controlled, clipped, miniature if not in its plants then in its imitation of landscape. Again he felt clumsy as he followed the old man along a twisting little path, his clothes becoming wet from brushing against the clipped green shapes. He took out his camera and crouched down, and photographed the vistas of the design, each angle too contrived to his eye, intensely artificial though he could not but appreciate the craftsmanship of the gardener. He took a couple of shots, and then stood, but the old man stayed watching him, so he took other shots, and walked back to the steps of the house and took a general picture of the bushes like posed figures, and the old man posing equally still among them.

It was good that you spent so much time in his garden, Kumiko said when they left. He loves it when people admire his garden.

It was raining again as if it had never ceased. Then there was the train again, the roofs that seemed to stretch all the way from Kamakura into Tokyo. The thing that my grandfather cannot forget, she said, is the war. My grandmother was saying that he remembers that now and forgets everything else. He was in the jungle and it was very terrible. Sometimes I think that that is why he likes to make his garden so tidy like it is.

There was a pause then as they listened to the train, and the train stopped at a station and passengers moved past them and got out, and others got in. And then she said, He fought against the British.

In Burma?

She nodded, head straight up and down like a toy. She was not to know there was any emotional significance in that for him.

Did it make them closer, or further apart?

She sat with the red raincoat open and falling back from her clothes, warm as he was warm from being wrapped up in the warm rain.

When we get to Shinjuku, will you come home with me?

The windows were open all through the house. The rain outside fell light and straight as it had fallen through almost all of the day. The street was shiny and black with the wet. In the gardens the bamboos sagged with the weight of water, even the hard leaves of shrubs had drooped and softened. The rain was so pervasive that within the house all of the surfaces, the paper of the screens and the straw of the tatami, had soaked up moisture. Everything was soft, moist. They made love with the windows slid open and the rain falling, and their bodies were hot and damp.

They heard the softened sounds of the world outside in the rain, the hush of the rain falling and their own breaths loud against it. They would have liked to have gone out into the rain and felt it on their skins, cooler than the dew of their sweat, streaming off their bodies as it had streamed from the stone folds on the Great Buddha, soaking into their skin, not pouring off it, because they were made of porous flesh and not of stone, washing them away.

Rain

In Kamakura also the rain kept falling, pouring down the roof and coming off it like a veil, running in streams between the little trees and down the twisting path. That rain that seemed so good to them had no mercy on the old people. It soaked into their kimonos, plastered their thin hair to their skulls and made them cold inside. The old man went out into it, and his wife followed when she saw that he was gone, she in her alarm going out without a coat, as he had gone without a coat in his vagueness, though at least, she would say, she could put on the gumboots she kept on the platform by the garden door.

My grandfather was strange after we left that day, Kumiko would tell him. She would not tell him this until some time later, after she had gone there when her grandfather was ill. Perhaps we stayed too long. We made him too excited. My grandmother says that he has the same schedule every day, a long sleep in the afternoon, but our visit had kept him up, and then after we had gone he would not sleep. You must be tired, she said, those young people will have tired you out. But no, he must go into the garden.

It's raining again, she said. Have a sleep now and I'll go out with you later. We can go out together when the rain stops.

The old woman persuaded him into his chair, and left him with the television on for company, but later on she looked in and found the room empty and the doors pushed wide open to the pouring rain. She told her granddaughter how she found him then, kneeling among the bushes with his hands full of soil, staring at his muddy hands and then tipping them over to see the soil fall back from his fingers, how there was mud on his face washed down it by the rain, and when she made him stand there was mud on his knees, and then all down his wet clothes when he wiped his hands on them. How she was soon as wet as he was, wet through as she chivvied him in, tugging him alongside her, her delicate frame alongside his bony one, matching her quick small steps to his slow ones, helping him indoors, making him change out of his clothes before she could change her own.

It must have been full day when they woke but they would hardly have known it. The slight movement of the wind chimes outside sounded thinly through the paper screens before the windows. Even when she pushed back the screens the light was veiled by the moisture in the air.

She stood, naked, and looked about his room. He watched her from the bed on the floor.

It's very empty, she said. You have no things. Only the camera.

I was travelling. You don't want too many things when you're travelling.

Then she pushed open the door to a cupboard that was full of a woman's clothes.

Whose clothes are these?

Laura's. I said I didn't need the cupboards so she could leave her stuff where it was.

She is your girlfriend?

No. He reached out for her.

If you have no things, then how do I know who you are?

She pulled back the sheet that covered him. She would know him in that moment only by his skin. She touched him then. She touched the paleness of his body, the faint lines of his tan which seemed to make him more naked than herself, the proof on him that there were places which she might touch where the sun had not.

Tell me what it's like where you come from.

I said before, it's flat countryside, you wouldn't think anything of it. No mountains. I don't know if you have any places in Japan like that.

Maybe some places in Hokkaido.

Have you been to Hokkaido?

I don't want to talk about Hokkaido. I want to know about you.

He spoke softly. She was lying on his chest. He had his hand on her hair. She would know the breath and the vibration of his words besides the sounds.

I have a brother and a mother and we live on a farm out in the countryside in the east of England. My brother does the farming –

What about your father?

He died when I was a child.

She raised her head to look at him. I'm sorry. He stroked the black of her hair and she rested on him again.

You should see it at harvest time. Then it is beautiful, all gold as far as you can see.

Like in America? In the movies. Like where Dorothy comes from in *The Wizard of Oz*?

No, not like America either. Like England, that's all. There's a farmhouse that's been there almost as long as America's been America, and a village and a church that have been there longer.

Do you have photos?

No photos. It's not special. It's just ordinary.

She looked into his eyes again. Will you go back there when you leave Japan? Help your brother on the farm?

No, I shouldn't think so. It's Richard's thing, not mine.

And it was your father's thing.

I suppose so. He didn't grow up on a farm though. He came there after he left the army. He could have gone to university or something, but they said now that the war was over the farmers would be the heroes.

That's good.

Was it good? I don't know if it was good.

Gently, he shifted her head from his chest and went to the kitchen to make coffee. He looked out of the window. A fine rain. Figures on the street beneath umbrellas. If he was alone he would have taken some pictures. Cartier-Bresson would have taken those pictures, the relationships between the umbrellas on the street and the spaces between them. He would have found the moment when the arrangement was perfect.

When he came back with the coffee she had dropped off to sleep again. He put down the two mugs and took up the camera instead. He photographed her splayed across the futon with only a piece of the bedding on her and her legs dropping above the tatami floor. He photographed her little feet that hung as if they were dancing above their shadows on the mat, her head and shoulders emerging from the white of the sheet, her face with the black hair falling across it, her mouth cracked open, darkness like a whisper between her lips. The photographs would be very soft because he used no flash.

Then he put the camera down, unsure of his right to take pictures of her like that while she slept. Her sleep made her closed to him, closed and apart, and he longed for her to wake. Yet when he put the camera down he did it gently, resting it on the cushioned black strap so that it did not make a noise to disturb her. He lay on his back on the futon beside her and closed his own eyes but did not sleep, his mind working over what, in a rush of openness, he wanted to tell her, what he might have told in that moment if only she had woken, lying beside him looking not at him but up to the neutrality of the ceiling, what would have opened him to her, sidelong, as he did not open to anyone; if she had not slept, if she had been able to see what he saw against the blankness; if, after all, she had not been Japanese. But she was soundly, innocently asleep, and she was Japanese, so how could he do anything other than keep it to himself?

Home. The farmhouse a ramble of older beamed rooms behind a regular brick facade, the front rooms tall and light with their sash windows, those at the back dim with small leaded casements. Two staircases, one from the hall and one from the kitchen; another narrow dusty set of stairs leading to the attic. How do you describe that kind of house to a Japanese? The size and age of it; the extent of the farm-yard, the old cowsheds and stables and barns in disrepair, Richard's new barns beyond them. And then the land, in which the farm itself was the dominant feature, that and the village and the church a half-mile off across the fields.

He wished that he did have pictures. Here is my house, he might have said, here is the garden where we used to play. Here my mother, my brother. No, he doesn't look like me. He's tall and fair. He looks more like my father. I take after my mother. Richard takes after my father, in temperament, people say, as well as looks. I suppose that's true, if they say it – but I was so young, I have only a notion of him. Here is my room – yes, we each had our own rooms, the house is big, with bedrooms to spare. This is the view from my window – my window looked out the back across the farm-yard to the fields. He would have shown her the pictures and tried to describe a childhood very different from that of a Japanese girl born in the same year in a suburb of Tokyo.

When I woke in the mornings – I always woke early – I would go straight to the window and look out and see what was going on.

There was more that he would have to tell her, if she was to understand, that could only be told and not shown in photographs. Because there was movement in it, and smell and sound, and continuity, the passing of time.

*   *   *

There was the work, that was a constant of the place. His father up and out often soon as it was light, the clank of machinery and engines starting up in the yard. The knowledge of his big and slightly stooped figure moving about, taking the tractor out, of the preoccupation that was a constant beneath his action, the thought of things past and things always about to be done. Then after his father was not there any more, the sound of contractors working the land, bringing in their own machines, so that the farm sound was outside-world noise, not belonging to the house; and now it belonged again, and there was Richard, a little later in his rising perhaps than their father had been, more systematic in his work, with the modern methods and the bigger machines that had made the new barns necessary.

There was the growing-up of boys on a farm. The naturalness of it, the occasional hardness, his mother who must have come to the farm urban and soft seeming somehow separated in those days, before; indoors most of the time as she had not begun to do the garden then, telling them to take off their boots when they came in; having wanted, perhaps, some quite other life. There was so much they did that they did not tell her about, of which she would have disapproved or been afraid.

There were the three of them, himself and Richard and their father. In the yard. Beside him riding on the tractor.

The three of them walking out to scare the pigeons from the fields. Shouting in the fields, whirling round as small living scarecrows. Scaring the crows which their father said were cleverer than the pigeons as the crows would peck into the ground all along a line of drilled seed. Standing still beside their father in the spinney when he shot the pigeons as they came in to roost, very still because the pigeons would spot them if they made the slightest movement, watching the birds come, waiting until their father had his shot. And then when Richard was old enough to have the .410, standing envious of the gun and of the wonderful responsibility and the paternal attention that were acquired by carrying it.

Boys, I need to tell you something.

She gathered them on the sofa in the sitting room, placing herself at the centre, he on one side of her, Richard on the other. She would have put her arms around them but the dog came up and nosed against her knees so she narrowed and her hands went to the dog instead.

Your father's had an accident.

Her touch only made the dog more restless.

He tripped, she said, with his gun. He had been climbing a fence and he tripped, and the gun went off.

Daddy shouldn't have done that, Richard said. Richard had been taught the rules: how to carry a gun, how you don't point it at anyone, how you don't carry it loaded, how you break it before you climb a fence.

Out After Dawn

He didn't say anything. His brother spoke but he did not speak. He did not speak because he had seen. So had the dog, which turned its head to him now, a retriever with brown pools of eyes and a slobbery mouth and pink tongue. The dog nuzzled into his lap, and he bent over and buried his head in its smelly golden coat. The dog had seen and whined over the form of the man on the ground, which was a form that was to be recognised by the clothing and the build and the hands but not by the head that was no longer a head but had fallen back into a heap of leaves, smearing with red the winter's wet leaves that were turning from copper to black as they lay. Coming between the trees the boy saw the dog and the man, and the shotgun which the man had clasped to him. He saw it only for an instant and ran away.

He ran back the way that he had come.

He ran back, and from that moment it all went in reverse. If only it could have been reversed, all of it, rolled back and rerun some other way.

He had come from the house. He had heard his father going out the back door. From his window he had seen his father walking out into the grey of the yard, with the dog beside him and his coat on and his tweed cap, and the gun under his arm. Everyone else was asleep. Richard was asleep in the next room. He had dressed quickly and gone down the back stairs, quietly so that he didn't wake them, and put on his own coat and went out too. If he ran, he might catch up. If he caught up, he would be walking in that still time after dawn, just himself with his father and the dog. So he had run the way that he thought that his father and the dog had gone, but he couldn't see them any more because of the fog. He had run out after them into the fog, across the paddock and then across the plough which was frosted and hard going. It was when he was halfway across the plough that he had heard the shot – and now when he was halfway back he heard a man shouting. Someone else had been out that morning, Billy Eastmond from the village gone to check his traps. Billy had rabbit traps on the Six Acre. He also would have heard the shot and wondered who was shooting in the fog.

It was Billy Eastmond who brought the dog and the news home.

She woke a second time and opened her eyes to see him. He was aware of her eyes on him. It was brighter now. The rain must have stopped and the sky cleared.

She was curled and warm with the sleep. She put out her hand to him where he lay so straight. Hello.

Hi.

What is it? Why do you stare at the ceiling like that?

It was just an ordinary wooden ceiling, directly above them the standard square light fitting made of paper and bamboo with a cord that could be pulled once or twice for different levels of light.

When he didn't turn his head her finger travelled all the way down his profile, down his forehead and his nose – his English nose, she said it was, though he didn't know what made a nose English – to his lips and over the turn of his chin.

What time is it?

Don't know. Must be late.

It's not raining.

No.

Let's get up and go to the park.

He made coffee again and they ate some toast which was all there was.

Which park? he asked. This one here?

No. A big park. Shinjuku Gyoen.

He took a picture of her on the way, in the street; another on the station platform when they were waiting for the train, her smile and the bright red raincoat making her stand out against the crowd. Why did you take that picture? she asked, and he said that he always took pictures in the stations. He planned a series of them: a particular view of Tokyo, the platforms, the tunnels, the ticket halls, the underground malls. Tokyo underground, she said. Yes, he said, that's right.

Then he took a picture of her in the train.

Is that for your series?

Wait and see.

Kumiko in the park, on the bridge above the lake, with her back to the trunk of a pine and the lake behind her, in front of a pavilion, beside a stone lantern, doing a star jump in the lime avenue in the French garden – big grin, legs wide, arms out in a line from her shoulders. He recorded so many instants of that day. But he was only doing what others did. Taking pictures was one of the things that Japanese couples did on Sundays in the park.

The next day when he saw her at work she was the girl with whom he had spent the weekend but she was also someone else. She was at the desk in reception, typing. She couldn't keep the smile out of her face and she seemed to be making a lot of mistakes, stopping her typing to white them out, reaching forward so that hair hung over the machine, tongue touched to her lips.

She was wearing crazy clothes, a miniskirt with a zigzag pattern on it.

I like what you're wearing today.

It's Monday. You have to be positive on Mondays. There's a whole five days to get through before the weekend.

That's true.

Shall we go somewhere this weekend?

How about tonight?

I can't do tonight.

Tomorrow night?

She shook her head. Too busy.

Wednesday then? The weekend seemed too far off.

Richard

It must have been sometime later that winter, maybe days later, maybe weeks, he doesn't know. A quiet moment, Richard not threatening this time. They were alone, by the tree in the garden that they used to climb, where their father had put a rope so that they could get up to the first branch. It could not have been a very wintry day because they were out climbing the tree.

I know you were there. You saw.

Where?

Tell me what happened.

I didn't see anything happen.

Richard didn't understand that what he said was true. He was there but he was late, and nothing happened when he was there. It was over. He was behind the action, crossing the bare field, walking into the aftermath of action and not into the action itself so that the action would never be explained. He could no more say how it happened than he could have made it not-happen.

When he got there, things were still. Fixed. Silent. There wasn't even a bird in the spinney, nothing rustling. The birds would have flown away with the shot. There wasn't a bird nor a fly nor anything else that moved. There was only the dew, glistening, and where there wasn't dew there was the red stain seeping from the leaves onto the soil, and the soil blotting it up.

4

Summer

*The pictures of summer have deep shadow in them as well
as light. The brown shadow that draws the eye to it from
the heat, from the gold of tatami in sunlight or from the green
of bamboos or the blue of the sky. The black shade beneath the
dark branches of pines. The charcoal shade beneath a roof. The
crisp double-barred outline of a torii thrown onto the ground
before a shrine. There are fewer pictures of the streets. Too
bright they are, too hard and hot to contemplate, the walls of
glass and concrete, the girls bare-armed and bare-legged, the
men removing their jackets, black and white in the sunlight.*

*In his pictures of the underground, neither the light nor the
scene changes, but only the clothes – the skimpiness of them and
the brighter range of colour, and perhaps a fatigue that shows
on men's and women's faces as they come down from the stifling
city above.*

It had become the hot Japan that he had used to imagine
before he came there, hot and humid. It was the humidity that made the days so heavy, the same humidity that

kept the leaves in the gardens outside his window so glossy green, that hung in the air and held the pollution low over the streets and closed off the sky. It made time slow. The sound of the wind chimes seemed to slow and die. The sound of the neighbours seemed no more than a rustle, all the sounds of the city distant and dulled. Some of his students went away, and his lessons reduced so that he had more of the day to himself, though he didn't use it to go out and take more pictures but too often stayed home in the flat in Inokashira, turning the fan up high and looking through whatever work he had developed, wondering if it would amount to anything. In the evenings if he did not see Kumiko he went to his regular bar and drank from his bottle there in the Japanese style, in a long glass with a quantity of crushed ice and cool water, smoking white-tipped Mild Sevens one after the other, topping up the glass so that it never emptied and stirring to see the dark gold of the whisky pale as it mixed. When he left the bar the night would still be sultry, black beyond the lights and lanterns of the street, but soothing like a black river taking him home, out of the entertainment district and through the park, over the lake, past the place where a bullfrog croaked, where each time he passed the bullfrog surprised him, even when he had come to anticipate it, and each time he thought again how comical it was that a frog should make such a bovine noise, that stood out against the background of the cicadas which seemed as much a part of the night as the darkness.

He slept heavily at first those nights, and then he would wake and throw the sheet off him, and lie and feel for the air coming off the fan. Or get up and drink a glass of water.

On the nights when she stayed with him it was too hot to sleep close. They made love and then they separated, and each knew the hot length of the other spread alongside though their bodies no longer touched.

This was how I used to think Japan would be, he said to her, from when I first heard of it, when I was a child. He had heard the word Japan and he had pictured a hot place, and nothing that he had learned about it since had altered that childhood expectation, not even the coming there and finding it cold.

And is England cold and rainy like I think it is?

Only some of the time.

There was a pause. His thoughts ran against the whirr of the fan. It was because of his father, he thought. Some mistaken childish logic. His father had fought the Japanese, in the war. He knew that because his mother had told him. His father did not speak of it but his mother had told him, later. His father had fought a dreadful war in the jungle – not in Japan of course, his father had fought in India, Assam, Burma, not Japan, but that did not matter to a boy. His mother said that he never got over it. He fought the Japanese in the jungle. The jungle was hot. Japan was a hot place.

Nowhere's quite like you picture it, he said, his voice spinning away into the darkness and the whirr of the fan.

Did she hear that, or was she already asleep? He felt a calm in the room, a sense that he was awake alone.

*   *   *

95

And her grandfather must have fought on the other side; his father young, just out of school, her grandfather a much older man.

And here were the two of them lying just so much apart beneath the fan.

He thought of the old man tending his bonsai, watering and feeding, training and pruning each one of his trees with exquisite care, removing the plants from their pots when the time came and pruning the roots, controlling the growth that could not be seen under the soil as much as the growth above. He thought of him bent in his brown kimono, the wrinkled skin on his bony turtle head, the precision of his hands and the wandering of his mind.

In the morning he said, How is your grandfather?

He's not well. He was in the hospital.

You didn't tell me.

It was after we were there. He caught a chill from going out in the rain.

She told him how he had gone out after they left and inexplicably filled his hands with soil.

He's back home now. My mother has gone to help look after him.

And his trees?

Oh yes, she will look after his trees.

Thunder

U sually it was Richard he played soldiers with. But
Richard was at school, and his mother had gone to
fetch him. The thunder cracked above the house.

Quick, Japs!

His father pushed him under the table. A big rough hand
on top of his head pushing him down, hectically so that
he bashed his elbow against the table leg. Then his father
crouching beside him, and the dog, standing, agitated. It
was the big table in the kitchen, a pine table with turned
blue-painted legs, and the paint on them was scuffed, and
there was a single wide drawer at one end that hung down
below the table top. He fitted under it easily, even where
the drawer was. Often he shared the space with the dog.
It was warm and close to the Aga, and there was a blanket for the dog, and no one trod on you there. But now
the dog was standing and moving round and round and
whining, mewling, and his father was too big. His father
under the table was hunched like the picture he had seen of
Alice when she drank the DRINK ME bottle and grew too
tall and pressed against the ceiling, but more so, all too-big

and bent, and crushed at the same time, his knees bent, his head down beneath his shoulders, crowding out the space with the size of his body and with his smell, which was sharper than the smell of the dog, not comforting like the smell of the dog but the opposite of comforting. His father held his two arms tight in his hands. Let go. You're hurting me. But he didn't let go, and they listened to the thunder again, so close to the house. And when the thunder had been gone some time his father's hands loosened. Can I go now? I want to pee. He did, terribly, want to pee. And he did not want to play this game, whatever it was that they were doing there, underneath the kitchen table. He got up, and the dog moved with him, brushing against his legs. He was in a terrible hurry so he only glimpsed, out of the corner of his eye as he ran out, the giant's body unravelling itself from under the table.

They each took a few days' holiday and went to the sea. Kumiko's uncle had a house in a village on the Izu peninsula. It was a long journey from Tokyo, first on a train and then on a bus, in and out of bays and villages along the rocky coastline, with the sea appearing to their right and occasionally a view across it to the mainland and to Fuji there. The villages were fishing villages, and there were boats and the people gathered seaweed and spread it on the beaches to dry, but they were farmers as well and worked small terraced fields where the land rose steeply behind. He saw them from the bus. He saw modern Japanese on holiday in Western casual clothes, and most of them were young, and he saw the fishermen and the farmers, who were almost all of them small and old and bent, old Japanese wearing patterned indigo-dyed pyjamas bent further under bamboo baskets which they carried on their backs, the young and the old threading between each other as if the other did not exist. He saw that he could take some very different pictures here. And the light, even though it was summer, was good, free of the haze of pollution.

The house was a modern one set up above the old village which clustered close to the shore. Kumiko's uncle was a successful businessman and had built the house as his company's holiday home. It seemed to have been scarcely touched by whoever had come there before them. There were fresh tatami rooms smelling of straw, and a balcony with a view to the sea, very few things in it but only clean bare space.

It's beautiful here, he said. He walked onto the balcony with his camera and took a first shot of the village roofs sloping steeply below, and across them the deep blue of the sea, and two great rocks that stood out of the sea in the centre of the little bay with a shrine upon them; a tall red torii on the summit of one of them and a swag of sacred rope slung across to the other. The mainland beyond was barely visible. Fuji should be there, Kumiko had said, but Fuji had quite gone. Perhaps in the morning when the air was fresh he would see it, and then he would take the shot again, and then the picture, with the foreground of roofs, and the positioning of the rocks and the rope and the torii, and Fuji in the far distance, would be a perfect view of Japan like one of Hiroshige's views.

Or they might swim to the rocks. She said that you could swim to the rocks, if you were a strong swimmer, and there were steps so that you could climb to the torii or to where the rope was fastened and dive back into the sea.

Then they went down into the village to buy some food, and he stopped on the path and took other Hiroshige views, of the houses and the bay, and the mountain at the end of the bay that jutted out into the sea as a single vast black and jagged rock, and which also had a shrine and a torii on its summit. After they had eaten, very late, they went out again and walked all the way up there. They walked again through the village that was empty and silent, and if Kumiko had not known the way they would not have found it. There was a narrow path between trees and stone lanterns, and then steps up steeply through a series of torii, and the path wound about and they could barely see the steps in the night. When they got to the top the moon was high and bright, though far from full, and they stood in the warm black night at the edge of the rock and looked down on three sides to the sea, and the sound of it came to them, and the far splash of white where it broke against the rock perpendicularly below.

Always she slept longer than he did. He had heard it said that it was a part of the art of being Japanese, the ability to sleep so easily. That a Japanese can get onto an underground train and be asleep before the first stop and yet wake in time for his or her destination. He did not know if that was true, he thought that sometimes they must sleep overlong, miss their stop and wake dazed and rush out and cross the platform and return down the line, but certainly they slept, that he had seen. Kumiko slept easily, and loved to sleep, and he loved her while she was sleeping. He loved the arrangement of her limbs, small, neat limbs neatly arranged even when she was unconscious, and the confusion of her hair falling across them.

He was sitting up, one foot off the mattress to the floor. Her hand caught his arm. I am not asleep, she said but her words were drowsy. Why must you get up so soon?

I've never been here before, he said. I want to go out, see the place.

Wait a little. Then I'll come with you.

He pushed back the paper screens from the window. There was the slope of the roofs once more, and the sea and the rocks and the torii, and in the far distance the tip of Fuji above the horizon where it seemed disconnected from the land.

It's very clear, he said.

It's too bright.

She had her arm across her eyes. The light from the open window streaked across the floor to where she lay. He pushed the screen halfway back.

That's better.

There are so many early-morning pictures. It is hard to distinguish, except by looking at the sequences in the negatives, when or in what order they were taken. The ones from Izu can often be identified by the crispness of their surroundings: in the new house the translucent paper of the screens is a brighter white, the tatami more golden, the bedding new and smooth, the light seeming brighter, all the contrasts sharper than in his old worn Tokyo flat. But the subject and the compositions remain the same. Kumiko sleeping. Kumiko fully asleep or half awake. Skin and hair and shadow. Her bare feet, her shoulder, her outstretched arm, her breast exposed by the fall of the cotton

yukata which she has put on to go and make tea and in which
she has gone back to sleep; her hand reached out at the edge of
the mattress and the white porcelain cup in a stripe of sunlight
on the floor beside it. Looking back, looking over them, he can
almost smell the tatami again and he can almost smell the sex.

She made breakfast. It was very simple, consisting of what
they had brought with them or what they could buy in
the shop in the village: juice, fresh peaches that she sliced,
coffee, toast, English marmalade which she had bought in
Tokyo. For you, she said, placing the jar on the table on the
balcony. You do like marmalade, don't you? She was still
wearing the yukata, which was not hers but belonged in the
house. It was a typical summer kimono, white with a traditional printed pattern of blue flowers. But her Japanese-
ness went so much deeper than that. It was in her bones, in
the precision in her movement, in the way she placed her
feet on the floor and in the way she moved her hands and
the way she held her cup in them. And in her eyes. It was as
if he could see where she ended, in what she was contained,
where some line was drawn or some invisible glass case was
set about her, defining and separating so that something
within her remained intact which he would never quite
touch. It made her the more beautiful to him in her sepa-
rateness, and it kept him intact also, also untouchable; each
of them within themselves and apart from the other. He
picked up the camera from the table top and took pictures
of her again, even when she sat down to eat. Don't do that

now, she said, and though she spoke with a smile he saw that she meant it, deeply. The lens separated them further.

You always take pictures of me.

But I like to take pictures of you.

He put the camera down on the table beside the orange juice and the marmalade. She put her hand on it, fingers spread, as if it were a threat to be gently covered over.

You take them all the time. You are always looking.

What else should I do?

I don't know, she said, removing her hand. Just be. Don't look, just be. And she turned her head down, away from him, and began to take the plates from the table and carry them inside.

When we go to the beach today, please don't take your camera.

So they went to the beach camera-less, and they were there before almost anyone else. And they went swimming together, and they found that they each of them swam well, and they swam out to the rocks in the centre of the bay, and they sat there for some time, high on one of the rocks, and watched as others came out and spread their towels on the beach, and Jonathan was glad that his camera was in the house and that he did not have to worry that anyone would come and steal it, for all that this was Japan and that things did not get stolen here. Then they swam back, and dried in the sun and put on their clothes and went for walk. She said they could walk to a cove along the coast where they might have the sea all to themselves. They walked out through the village along a concrete road until the road ended, and then along a track, up between terraced orange groves. The day was hot and yet the heat was not oppressive as in the city. There was a breeze, and there was the open sky and the sight of the sea behind them.

They met a farmer on the path, old, bent, bow-legged.

You don't see young farmers, he said. Don't these people have children?

Of course they have children.

Then why is it the only the old people we see working?

I guess the young ones have gone to the city.

So what happens when the old people get too old and die?

They come back, I guess.

They come back and get like their parents?

I don't know. I guess so.

Once there had been more fields than there were now. As they went on up the path he saw that they were walking between the outlines of abandoned terraces, overgrown now with cane and dry summer grass, and loud with crickets. They walked on in the heightened sound of the crickets and met no one else until they came upon the monkey. They had come to a dip in the land, and then there was a steep and rocky rise towards the ridge above the sea. There was a colony of monkeys that lived there on the ridge, and they saw the monkeys up ahead, grey forms moving among the rocks, and he thought nothing of it, and they walked past a group of them, and the monkeys were just being monkeys, playing, chewing cane, picking with their long fingers in the stones, a mother running with a baby clinging to the fur of her back, but then they came upon this particular monkey, and coming upon it was not like seeing an animal, it was like a meeting. The monkey stood across their path and glared at them, and there was intelligence in his eyes, and he seemed to challenge them on a human level, eye to eye, teeth bared in his long pink face.

For a moment, they stopped.

I don't like it, she said.

They took another step forward, and the monkey let them pass.

It was the one jarring moment in the day, which until then had been so beautiful. It was only a moment – they stopped for that moment and then they walked on, together, and the monkey ambled sullenly aside – but it stayed with them. They walked on and went down to the cove she had mentioned, and it was spectacular, and if he had had his camera he might have taken spectacular if clichéd photographs, such as so many others would have taken before him, of the sea and the spray on the rocks, and a huge rock out in the bay that had a tunnel through it where they saw a speedboat pass, and the speedboat's wake fanning behind. But he didn't have his camera, and they didn't remain there. There were too many monkeys around, and the monkeys made it ugly. They only looked, and then they climbed back up the cliff, and walked on, further than they had planned, and it became a long hot circular walk that took them eventually back to the village late in the afternoon.

*   *   *

I don't like those monkeys, she said. Of all the things they talked about that day, this was the conversation he would remember. There's that selection process at work always: what you see and what you listen to, and what you remember, and so often what you select reflects what is already seen or heard or remembered somewhere in your mind. They were coming down through orange groves again, the sea before them. She walked sometimes ahead of him, sometimes alongside. They had been walking too long, longer than they had meant to, and they were thirsty and hot. She was wearing brief denim shorts and a pink T-shirt with something meaningless written on it in English: Live Human Life. She had her hair knotted away from her face but strands came loose and fell forward across her forehead or her cheek, and now and then she put up her hand to push them back, and sometimes they clung because her forehead was sweating. My grandfather won't come here any more because of the monkeys. He used to come here, and he liked it then and didn't mind, but he won't come any more. My uncle wanted him to come last year for Golden Week. He wasn't so sick then, it would have been easy for him to come. He would have come with my grandmother, so that it would be a rest for her, and my cousins would be here, all their other grandchildren, and they would have a holiday together, but suddenly my grandfather was afraid of the monkeys.

They remind him of the jungle, she said.

She said many other things but this was what he would remember. He would remember it in another layer of his mind, apart from everything else to do with her.

My grandfather was old to be in the army. He was older, so maybe he saw more, saw the truth. And where he was, it was very bad. I think that he knew before the rest of the Japanese that Japan would lose the war. They lost in a terrible battle. Then they walked for weeks through the jungle in the rain, cutting through it and crossing great stormy rivers. Now, he speaks sometimes of this. He did not speak of it before. I know that it rained and rained, and they were sick and starving, and thousands of them died.

Did I tell you, when I went to see him last week he thought I was my mother? He called me by my mother's name, and my grandmother had to tell him who I was, that I wasn't Noriko but Noriko's daughter. It's me, Kumiko, I said. Then he said of course it was. He said it was just a slip of the tongue, he knew all along. It wasn't true. He didn't know. He had forgotten. He forgets who we are, but he remembers the war.

He didn't speak. He walked alongside as she spoke, walked in step, listened to her voice, felt her beside him and let his own thoughts run.

That's it, he thought. War is the most concrete thing. The memory of war will stay with a man longer than anything else. Hard and vivid. Stronger, so much stronger, than anything else he will ever know.

He paused a few moments to look at the view, fell back as she walked on. Her pink T-shirt waited for him beside a rock, her smile a challenge when he reached her. She ran then, and he must run after her, down the steep path through the terraces. They stopped where the path became steps and there was a little shrine, a standing rock and a stone figure of a god, and a small everyday sake jar with wilted flowers in it before the god, and a long way below them was the village, and beyond it the sea.

Shall we go for a swim?

No, he said. He felt dull, drained, his head beginning to throb. Let's just go home.

But she turned to him with her bright smile. There was such brightness in her even after the too-long walk, persuading him.

But they will all be going from the beach now. We'll have it to ourselves.

The beach was almost empty again, and the sea was soft in the evening and washed away the dullness and the sweat, and when they went back and made love later they could taste the salt on each other's skin. As if they were shells, she said, licking the hollows of shells.

Jungle

The night was oppressively hot, even with the screens wide open on two sides of the room. He woke. At times they each of them woke, and tossed about. He got up at some point when all the room was grey, and went to the window to breathe a fresher air and look out to the paling sky and the glimmer of the sea, and when he went back to the bed she had spread further across it in her sleep. He couldn't see her face. There was the grey of the sheet, and against it the darkness of her hair and of her legs splayed across the bed, and he lay down on his side in the narrow space remaining to him and wanted to lift the sheet from her middle and see that there was no red wound there and see that she was whole. But that would wake her. He put his hand tentatively to the sheet over the place where the wound would have been.

Whatever he could imagine must be so much less than what was. The old man's horrors. The monkeys. What was it that made him afraid? That there were monkeys in the jungle? That men fought with teeth bared like monkeys. That he had seen teeth bared in anger or later bared in death on the jungle paths as lips drew back, so swiftly in the tropics, and decayed on other men's skulls. He lay there and thought of the horror. He had gone to find it for himself. He found another war in the jungle, a different war with its own, different horrors. He had meant to go in close, to see the eyes. That was what Capa said you had to do, to go in close. That was how you took the best pictures.

But you cannot photograph war, Capa said that too. (And Capa should know because Capa was the greatest war photographer of them all.) You could not photograph war because war was an emotion. How could you photograph an emotion?

She curled now in her sleep and gave him space. She was whole, and she slept deeply, and she had no knowledge of those things he had seen even when he saw them beside her. He fitted his body along the outline of hers, tried to breathe with her slow sleeping breaths.

The photographs she has taken of him show nothing of his dreams. The dreams must have passed with the night and now that it is morning he does not dream any more. He lies on his stomach and angled across the bed, taking up the whole of it so that it would seem that she had got up some time before and he has moved across and settled deeper into dream-less sleep since she had gone. He is naked – or possibly she has picked away the last of the sheet that covered him, and that is a part of the mischief he will see on her face when eventu-ally he wakes. One leg is stretched straight behind him, the other bent as if in running, the rise of his buttocks catching light and giving shade (even in close-up their maleness evident by the flatness of them and the dents in their sides). His body is turned a little in the direction of the running leg, the left shoulder blade angled and raised, the left arm falling to the edge of the mattress, the hand loose as if something has just dropped from it, the right arm flat and bent above his head upon the pillow. His face is turned to the left, to the sunlight which in the first of the pictures has just touched his forehead but which by the end of the series reaches all of his head and

112

his chest. He must have been sleeping very heavily at last if he has not been woken by the light.

He looks very young, even to himself when he sees the pictures developed. Perhaps it was the sleep. Sleep makes a person look younger. He seems strange to himself, like some boy he does not know. His body in repose seems that of a boy: the slight build, the tousle of brown hair, the defenceless back; his face in sleep a boy's face, pouting into the pillow. He had taken pictures of her like this, and she was both girl and woman in them, but in these pictures when nothing in him is tensed, nothing closed, he seems exposed as no more than a boy.

For once she has been awake before him, and she has taken up the camera and taken pictures ruthlessly, not only of what she finds beautiful in him, his English profile or the line of his spine, or his blunt, dangling hand, but also of his oddities, the freckles and moles and marks on his skin, all the tidelines of sunburn on him, where his swimming trunks ended, where his arms and the back of his neck were burned above his T-shirt on the previous day's walk.

He heard her moving, bare feet on tatami. He felt her shadow moving across him and heard the click of the camera. How long had she been doing this before he woke? For a moment more he indulged his passivity, abandoning himself to her eye as to the light. Then he reached for her. His hand so close to the edge of the mattress grabbed for her ankle. But she was too quick. She must have seen the thought coiling in him and dodged away. He stood up, growling, and she laughed and flitted out of the room, down the stairs and out of the door on to the balcony and into the sunlight where all of the village could see her. He couldn't follow because he had no clothes on, and she took more pictures of him at the door, half hidden behind it, reaching out one arm, laughing and calling her in.

There is that picture too, a whole strip of them, he looking absurd, his nudity and his erection variously hidden or not hidden by shadows and the door.

Later she made him let her take up the camera again. They had gone down to the beach together and had swum together, and then she had come back and lain on her towel while he stayed out in the water, swimming a long way out into the bay. When he came in she was lying there still, flat in the sun, and he took the camera from the bag beside her and went off down the beach taking pictures of the place. He had been thinking of that when he was in the water looking back at the shore, of the pictures he would take and the patterns that people made across the sand.

Let me take some pictures now.

Not of me, he said, holding the camera back. No more pictures of me.

Why not?

I don't like pictures of me.

OK, I won't take pictures of you.

So she took the camera and wandered off and she too took pictures of the waves, and of children playing with a ball, and when he wasn't watching her any more she came back and took some of him, using the lens to go closer. They wouldn't be much good as pictures. It was midday by then and the light was dazzling.

5
The American

The American's hair is so blond that the Japanese turn to look at him in the street. Walking behind him it was possible to catch the stares. Two schoolgirls in their bulky long-skirted uniforms giggle and clutch one another at the elbow as if they see a film star pass. A small boy, too young to have been trained not to, points, and his mother crouches and gently wraps her hand over his pointing one. He walks straight ahead, looking at no one, one thumb under the strap of the rucksack slung over his shoulder, his bright head above the crowd. He is tall and broad-shouldered. He has strong regular features. His look is fixed before him, tight, seeming to have no relation to the crowd. If it were not for those surroundings, the passing cars and the shop signs, he might be an athlete striding towards the gate at some sporting event – a rower, a tennis player, a thrower of the javelin, walking closed to the moment, within himself, psyching himself for the test ahead.

There are other pictures of him, a series of snapshots from the time they went hiking in the mountains, along the gorge at Chichibu Tama: more relaxed here, smiling – and yet isn't there still some restraint in the smile? – standing golden and alone before the jagged mountainside and the deep blue sky; or with Kumiko and the pretty girl he had brought with him whose name Jonathan couldn't remember, the two Japanese girls smiling beside him and the waterfalls behind; then in the crowded Sunday-evening train coming back into Tokyo, in more of the subway pictures, again the tall fair gaijin among the Japanese, followed through the maze of Shinjuku station as at the time when they first met.

The last photo shows him again with two girls, with the other girl Akiho and with Kumiko, beneath an umbrella at the hot spring that third and last of the days they spent together. He holds the umbrella over his head, tall above the girls who lean in close on either side of him. They are standing in front of the hotel, and the mountain landscape they had gone to see is lost in the rain.

There had been an inevitability to it, or so it seems to him now, looking back, looking through the photos: that they had each found their way to this city, which was a city to hide in and yet a city in which they found each other hiding. It was the biggest city in the world, a city of eleven million people, but gaijin made thin paths within it like the paths that animals make in the wild, and followed one another along them.

It had been one of those slow days. A Friday. Kumiko was going that evening to her grandparents'. The old man's condition had not improved but neither had it worsened, and Kumiko was going for the weekend to give her mother a break. He had no lessons scheduled so he had been in the flat much of the time, dully sorting things out, planning his teaching for the following week. Though he had the fan going and all the windows open it had been stifling. The outside air seemed drained of life as it was of colour, no movement in it to stir the wind chimes or to carry any specific sound out of the blur of the city. Inside, he had found himself doing little more than listening to the fan as it turned on its stem, waiting for it to direct its blast of air to where he sat. When at last he went out he switched off the fan but he left the windows open for the night to enter. To come back into the stale room would be to step back into his own boredom.

He went to the cinema. He saw the first English-language film he could find, a run-of-the-mill thriller just compelling enough to transport him into a clichéd urban America. When he came out it was dark. He had the images of the film still strong in his head so that the lights and the people on the streets and all the chaos of signs, the now-familiar disorientation of the Tokyo night, was overlaid by that of Los Angeles or whatever city it had been in the film.

A tall gaijin was walking ahead of him. Gaijin were so rare outside of Roppongi that he always noticed them. He would see them and wonder what had brought them, and be aware that they also would see him. Most gaijin were taller than the Japanese and stood out a long way off. He wasn't tall and yet he knew that sooner or later they saw him too. This man must have been sitting a few rows behind him in the film. He had stood up first, and gone before him down the aisle and out of the cinema doors, and now he found that he was following him in the street, realising that because of his height he might follow him through this city a long way, but it happened that he was going that way anyhow, going the same way that he was, following the blond head to the station entrance and down to the same platform, seeing him stop further along the platform to wait for the same train. An American, most likely, another English teacher. His hair was too long for a businessman, hair that was straw-blond in the lights of the station, that made his figure very distinctive. He looked, and the other looked back, and the sort of wordless acknowledgement passed between them that passed between gaijin, and it came to Jonathan that he must have seen him before but he couldn't think where. That bright hair was so distinctive.

The wait seemed longer than usual. There weren't many people on their platform. The platform opposite was crowded, then a train came in and it was left empty, and they stood and waited as others came and again filled the space. If the train had come sooner his thought might have passed and been forgotten.

They got on at different ends of the same carriage. He sat where he could see the other man down the carriage, sat opposite a prim girl and, beside her, the usual sleeping salaryman – grey suit, lolling head and open mouth, legs apart, slip-on shoes and white nylon socks. When he first arrived he might have taken the picture, the upright girl and the lolling man, a typical image of Tokyo underground, but by now he had a dozen variations on the theme. Eight stops to Kichijoji. The girl got up and left.

Each time they came to a stop the sleeping man seemed about to wake but settled back again. Along the carriage, the gaijin also seemed to be travelling all down the line, sitting still, head raised, looking ahead, looking at nothing. Around the seventh stop it came to him who he was.

He let him go first out of the carriage, down the platform, up the stairs and through the turnstile. He had intended to go straight home, which would have meant turning left when he got out of the station, but the other man turned towards the entertainment district and he followed. He had no plan in his mind, he just followed. He meant, he supposed, to know where the other man was going, just to know something, anything, about him. If they had coincided like this, then he must follow and not let him go without knowing something about him. He was walking down one of the narrow streets of the entertainment district, and following was easy. The street was full of pedestrians on a Friday night but the American was tall, head above the rest, and though it was night there were lights all down the street, neon lights and gleaming signs and red and white lanterns, and the golden head was easy to make out above the stream of black ones. He knew the street well, he walked it often, it was familiar ground. He might have walked it with his eyes closed and known where he was by the sounds and the smells of it, the bars he walked by and the games parlours and the restaurants. This must be familiar ground to the American also, he thought. He too must know where he was going because he didn't slow or look about him, for all the lights and the people and the things going on. He

cut through the crowd smooth and fast and directed, and
Jonathan followed, and then there was a moment when a
knot of men reeled out drunk from the door of a restaurant and separated them, and in that moment Jonathan
felt panic. He did not want to lose sight of this man, who
suddenly meant so much to him. He pushed his way
through, getting shocked looks from the Japanese as he did
so. And just when he thought he had lost him, there he was.
He had stopped at a doorway, and the two of them found
themselves suddenly alongside one another, and they were
looking at one another and speaking. The American spoke,
and he replied. Hi, I saw you at the movie. Do you want
to have a drink? I was going to go into this bar here but it
looks pretty crowded. Yes, he said, and then he said, no. He
said there was a quieter place up the street where he kept a
bottle. He suggested they went there instead.

What did you think of the movie?
    It passed the time.
    Not much choice here.
    You been here long?
    A few months. And you? How long have you been here?
    Since March.

I think I saw you once, the American said. In the park.
    Maybe that was it. That was all it was. Maybe he had
just seen him in the park.

124

I came here once before, the American said, looking around. Tried to find it again but I couldn't. There are so many of these little places hidden away.

Then they sat face-to-face, and he was sure. They sat down at one of the tables by the window, and the barman brought his bottle and two glasses, and set out crackers and water and ice before them. The hair was a distraction. It was the hair that had put him off. He hadn't seen the hair that first time, only the face, under the helmet. The face blackened and smeared with war.

My name's Jim, the American was saying. What's yours?

His face blackened and shocked and unshaven, his eyes blank.

Jonathan, he said. He had not thought until now that the man in his photograph had a name. Men in such photographs don't have names. They have some other meaning.

Is that what is says there on the bottle, in Japanese? *jo-na-tha-nu?*

I thought it would stick out in English.

They can read it, you know.

What? He had lost track of the conversation.

You can't read it, but they can. They can read it's an English name. Writing it in Japanese doesn't make you any more anonymous.

No, I suppose it doesn't. Of course it doesn't. I didn't think of that.

Yet he was. He was anonymous. He knew the American but the American didn't know him. Perhaps those eyes just weren't seeing anything when he stood before them and took the picture. Perhaps he wasn't seeing anything at all, or what he was seeing was what he had seen already, sights so much stronger than what was in front of him in that moment, than a man with a camera first standing, then crouching, before him. Or perhaps he saw the camera, but that was all that he saw. That's what people say sometimes, that the camera makes the photographer behind it invisible. And now the two of them had met, and one knew and the other didn't. One had stalked the other down the street, because there was something he needed to know, but now that they had met he didn't know what it was. He had the urge to leave, then and there, leave the bar and not come back to it again.

There had been no reason to stay so long. No reason to top up the American's glass, to drink to the end of that bottle and accept a glass then from the bottle that the American bought and on which he put his own name. (I'll write it, he said to the barman and gave it to him on a scrap of paper. It was a complicated spelling, Norwegian or Swedish, Jonathan thought, like his hair.) Even if that had been only politeness, and staying so late, inertia, an effect of the heaviness of the weather and the drink, and the purposelessness of the day just passed and of the weekend that was to follow, he need not have arranged to see him again.

What do you do? he had asked.

Teach English.

Same as he did. That signified nothing. It was what so many of them were doing – just a way of being there, or a way of not being somewhere else.

Why Tokyo?

A shrug. I'd been in Asia before. It's easy to find work here. How about you?

He might have said that he took pictures, but he had held back from saying that, in the circumstances. Jim was looking away, lighting a cigarette. The bar was busy on a Friday night, full of dark heads and smoke, a hum of voices, jazz playing; it wasn't necessary for them to talk all the time. Only the two seats beside them at the table were empty, a space the world put around them, and when they did talk it was as if they were talking over a well or into a cave, some black echoing space which expanded the significance of their words. He wished that someone would come and fill the empty seats, crowd them out. Jim was holding his glass, not drinking, his eyes looking somewhere across the bar. The light caught the pale whisky, the glass, the dark heads, the smoke, his golden hair, his blue eyes. Was the memory there in that moment, behind his eyes? Always there, like a kind of tinnitus? Or did it come only sometimes, in waves or in the night?

Are you from the city? I'm not from the city, Jim had said. His glass was back on the table, his cigarette almost burned down in his fingers, his eyes on the crowd. I don't think I could live in a city for ever.

Where are you from then?

Rural Iowa. He rolled the *rr*s to emphasise the strangeness of the rural here.

Are you farmers?

My father's a pastor.

Out in the countryside?

That's right. He stubbed out his cigarette and spoke as if there was something sad about it. Big skies, flat land. No people. Or just a few people and you know who they all are.

My family has a farm.

They're all farmers round where I come from.

Do you like it?

Yeah, I liked it. He looked around him. I liked the space.

I don't know, Jonathan said, I think I like it better here. They're small, aren't they, those places, even when the skies are so big? You know everyone but everyone knows you and everything that's ever happened to you.

Yeah, that's right.

They hadn't left until sometime after midnight. They parted casually. They exchanged numbers, and they said something about meeting on Sunday. They came down the stairs from the bar and turned in their opposite directions when they reached the street.

Once he was gone, he had wanted to turn back. He wanted to go back after him, and turn him around and touch him. Hold him between his two hands and tear. Tear him open and see what was inside, as if he would come apart in his hands like paper, torn white edges to him and nothing more. Then he would tear and tear again, taking the torn pieces, the coloured pieces from tonight and the black-and-white pieces from before, taking them again in his fingers and putting them together, and tearing them into ever smaller pieces, scattering them so that the images in them might never be reconstructed from the scraps. But he didn't go back. He just made his quiet way home. He walked through Kichijoji to the park, and he walked through the park, down the wide path beneath the trees, past the police box and over the bridge, a humpbacked oriental bridge of concrete cast in imitation of rustic wood, a toy bridge and a toy police box, with a toy policeman standing straight in his uniform with white gloves and white belt and strap across his chest and holster at his hip. If the other was true, then this wasn't. If this was true, then how could the other be? In peace it is best to believe that war does not exist. Toy street, toy houses, toy steps to his door, hot room with windows open. Turning on the fan. Lying on his bed on the floor, waiting for the moving air to brush him in the dark.

Where were you before you came here? He had dared to ask that.

I did a tour in Vietnam. Went home for a couple of months. Couldn't hack it back in the States. Came here.

There were lots of Vets in Tokyo, he said. An English person probably wouldn't notice that, but he did. He didn't seek them out but he knew them when he saw them.

His face was strong. That bone structure was why he had made such a good picture. His look should have been strong but it was evasive, never meeting yours for long. He looked away again, took a sip and swallowed as if the whisky was bitter, his hand tight on the glass.

They come here because it's halfway. It's still Asia but you can live in it. They come for the women. They want to be with Asian women. And they come because they can't face the people back home. They can't take the way people back home look at them.

He had thought he might have the dream again. But he didn't have the dream. Maybe he had had too much whisky for any dream. In the morning he took a picture of himself. Now and then he took these self-portraits, focusing the camera and then holding it beside or below his head, or sometimes before him across his face as he must appear to those others whose pictures he took. He could not have said precisely what moved him to do this at any particular time, only perhaps that they represented moments of introspection, that they were a sort of outward introspection. But he had not taken a picture of himself in a while – not, he thought, since he had been with Kumiko. With Kumiko, there was someone else to see him, to see him first and then sometimes, though they no longer mattered because of course she was there and he was no longer alone, to take the pictures. Perhaps he took the pictures at those moments when his identity was most unsure, when he was losing the sense of himself; as this morning, hung-over and unshaven, unsure of himself because he had made friends with a man he didn't want ever to have met, and moreover he had wanted for some reason to be liked by this man, or he had some need of him, so he had presented himself with part of himself omitted; he had presented only a surface to the man like the surface his lens recorded in the mirror. He put the camera before his face. It was no wonder the man did not know him. The camera hid him. And as soon as it did not hide him, he had turned away and run for the chopper. He had never looked at the soldier eye to eye but only through the viewfinder, compressed, reduced; as object rather than man.

There is the picture, himself in the cramped bathroom of the flat. The mirror is set low, at a Japanese height. If he were tall like Jim he would have had to bend his knees to get his head in. A slight, bleary figure. Undistinguished, insignificant. A non-combatant. Who would notice him?

I met a guy here, Jim had said, a Vet, with a terribly scarred face. I guess he'd had surgery, skin grafts, but still you could see that his face had been ripped apart. It was scarred on one side and perfect the other. One of his eyes was glass, but well made so you didn't see it at first. He liked it here. He said this place was kind to him. And it was. They didn't stare because of the scars, they stared only because he was a gaijin. He thought they accepted the way he looked along with the rest of him. That's a good thing about Japan. They don't see you here. You think they stare at you but they don't see you like they do back home. They don't question who or what you are.

*   *   *

You're free here. Back home you have to carry the war with you all of the time. People see you and they think they know something about you. You've got the war inside of you and you want to forget it and be like them, but you can't be like them and they aren't gonna let you anyways. Going home to people who only know peace might be the worst thing you can do when you have that inside of you.

He took the morning slowly. He did not have to meet him again. There had been that vague arrangement to meet to go to the museum in Ueno the following day, but he did not have to turn up. That would be best, he thought, if he just didn't go – or kinder to phone first and make some excuse – and then he wouldn't see him again. He went out to the shops, came back. Mrs Ozawa was watering the plants at the door to her house. *Ohayu.* He bowed to her and admired the morning glories that were trained up the wall beside his staircase. His mother planted the same variety. Heavenly Blue, they were called. Mrs Ozawa had trained them exquisitely, the stems on separate strings so that each flower stood out individual and perfect when its trumpet opened to the light. Back in his little kitchen he unpacked his simple groceries, lit the gas ring and boiled water for coffee. The kitchen just fitted a person on his own. Its window was a narrow rectangle onto a precise and orderly world. He took the coffee into the main room. He might have looked at the Vietnam pictures again but he didn't need to. He knew them well enough already.

Now and then he heard the village burning, felt it like a hot wind, or he took a breath and caught the smell of it as if it was some smell he had brought in from outside on his shoe, only he wasn't wearing shoes. The Japanese took their shoes off when they came in from outside. How sensible that was. After he had drunk his coffee he put on his shoes and took up his camera and went out.

He walked where the streets were quiet and he took pictures of things. He looked for what was beautiful, for those details where the Japanese aesthetic stood out perfect and calm, that you could almost always find if you looked, in the corners of the city. Mrs Ozawa's morning glories that set the colour of the sky against the dark wood of the wall. A neighbour's bamboo fence. Another bamboo fence with a workman's canvas footwear stuck on two posts to dry as if someone's feet were in the air. Blue and white yukata hung to dry on poles inserted through their sleeves like a line of cut-paper figures swaying in the breeze. There are many things a person sees, he thought, but a person has the choice of what he looks at. If he could train his eye, could he not see a different world?

I take pictures, he would tell the American the next day when they met. He would take his camera with him and go to meet him as they had planned – as perhaps he had meant to all the time, though he had been telling himself otherwise – and this time he would tell the American what it was that he did. Tokyo's a great place to take pictures. I take a lot in black and white. Tokyo's great in black and white. I take street pictures, and I take pictures of gardens. At the place where I live, my window looks out across gardens. I take a picture from that window every morning, every morning I look for the difference in the light. The light in the early mornings this time of year is much clearer than the light in the day. It throws long shadows, and some mornings more than others there's dew on the leaves. I like to take pictures in the early morning – like this morning, I went out very early, I was awake early, I didn't sleep very much last night, I had a lot on my mind. On mornings like today, I go out and I take pictures of the little gardens in the neighbourhood, where you can see in through the fences, and the fences are beautiful so I take pictures of those too. I take pictures in the park where you said you saw me – was I taking pictures then? That's a great place for pictures. You know those little turtles in the pond there? Have you seen how sometimes the turtles rest on the posts that jut from the water by the bridge and sunbathe with their legs sticking out from their shells? So relaxed they look like that, and safe, with the water all around them. And I go to the other parks, and the public gardens. There's a lovely garden at the Nezu Gallery. Have you been there? I have a girlfriend who takes me to gardens. She took me to view the irises in the gardens by the Meiji Shrine. She's in Kamakura this weekend. Her grandparents live in Kamakura. She took me to the Hydrangea Temple there but we were too early and they hadn't flowered yet. He would tell him all sorts of things like that.

135

It was an old museum of big rooms and small objects under glass in brown wooden cases. There was an exhibition of utensils used in the tea ceremony, people crowding round a case in the centre of a great room that held only a single cup, a brown cup so small that you might hold and hide it in the fingers of your hand, that looked as if it was formed in the fires of the earth. In another case, a teapot; a bamboo whisk. The objects were small and the ceilings were high, hung with calligraphy scrolls, whole poems or single inked words, black ink on white paper, mute and exquisite.

For a long time they stood before a screen that was painted with pine trees in a mist. And just when he felt that he had looked enough, when he had seen how the mist seemed to cling to the surface of the screen and the pines to recede into it, when he had taken in the composition, the relationship between each spare vertical on the long horizontal plane, when he had looked at the caption on the wall that was all in Japanese but he could read the era in which the screen was made if nothing else, just at that same moment Jim began to move on, and the two of them moved on together. It was not the sort of art about which he had anything to say, and neither of them said anything about it. He did not know if Jim had been drawn into contemplation as he had, or even whether he was interested, or whether he was only accompanying him, moving only as he anticipated his movement. What did he see, what did he like, what had he seen? He also was indecipherable. His eyes were alert, alive, and yet there was a stillness in his face. He could not tell if Jim was thinking of the pictures or of some other thing, something in his surroundings or something within himself.

And the air did not move in the great space of the gallery where they walked. The air seemed old as the things within it.

It's hot here, was all that he said.

Let's go out into the park.

He has a sheet of contacts from that visit to the park. He didn't take many shots that day and those that he did take weren't much good. There are a few of Jim. There is one of him by the lake in the park, then there are the ones he took in the street as they walked to the Asakusa Temple. He looks very handsome in the pictures. Kumiko would say how handsome his new friend was, when they met. That his friend looked like Paul Newman, Robert Redford and Peter Fonda rolled into one. Plus a touch of Clint Eastwood, she added, that cool shut-away look in him that was so sexy and male, and pulled the girls.

What did you do? she asked after that weekend she had spent away. They were walking down the street on their way to a restaurant for dinner.

I met someone, he said.

A girl? she said, her dark eyes on his, her little hands halted as she reached into her handbag for cigarettes.

No, not a girl.

Daijoubu. That's OK then. She tapped a cigarette from the packet and put her Mickey Mouse lighter to it. It wasn't conventional for a Japanese girl to smoke in the street. It was a mark of her freedom, like going out with a gaijin.

An American. We went to the museum at Ueno.

Ah, she said. It was clear that she thought the museum was boring. And would I like this American?

He's very handsome. Perhaps I shouldn't introduce you.

Doesn't he have a girlfriend of his own?

I think he does.

Then let's go somewhere together.

The next time they went on a trip they went with the American and the pretty, forgettable girl he brought along. It was Kumiko's idea. They took a train out of the city to Chichibu Tama. It was a pleasant day and they all said that they would come back in the autumn and do the hike again to see the colours for which the gorge was famous – though as it turned out they would have stopped seeing each other by then.

So what did you think of him? he said to her later.

She shrugged. I don't know. I don't know much about him. He's cool.

Her big teasing smile.

Am I not cool?

She laughed. And teased him then about the film stars.

On a shelf up behind the bar their keep-bottles stood alongside one another, two English names among the Japanese. Sometimes one bottle was taken down, sometimes the other. Sometimes they met there; other times they went alone. If he had not wanted to see Jim he would have had to find a new place, but he told himself that he liked this one, he was accustomed to it and he liked the kind of music they played. And perhaps when he came now it was even partly in the hope of seeing him, though they would speak now about no more than what he would speak about to other regulars, about the typhoon whose course was predicted to pass out beyond Tokyo Bay, or the form of the various star wrestlers in advance of the autumn sumo tournament. It often happens like that, he thought, that the first time you meet someone you talk hard and begin to tell one another about yourselves, and then once you know them a little you draw back into the day-to-day, which is so much easier said and reveals less.

The more that he saw of him, the less he felt that he knew him. In all their brief acquaintance, in the meetings in the bar, the couple of times they went to see films together, the two trips they took out with their girlfriends, he never learned so much about Jim as on that first night, when they had met by chance and had the freedom with each other of strangers who might never have to meet again. He saw that Jim had moods. He saw him talkative and full of charm one night, lighting up the bar with his blue eyes and his American smile, and silent another. On the nights when he was silent he looked into his glass, and stayed in the bar longer, drank longer. Don't you have to work tomorrow? he would ask, as he himself got up to leave, and Jim would be putting more ice in his glass or reaching for the bottle or lighting another cigarette. Only very rarely, as he remembered it, did Jim speak about what he did elsewhere, or about his work or his students, so that at times he wondered if there were any, or if Jim spent all of his days only drifting across Tokyo. But there was money in his wallet, and his clothes were good, and he kept a car which was more than most English teachers did, and once he mentioned a corporate language course in Nagoya, so there must have been work some of the time. What did it matter, he asked himself, what Jim did? Wasn't he drifting too?

The city improved as the humidity lifted. Places that had seemed a long walk away weren't far to go to any more. The sky cleared and even the sounds seemed clearer, that had been muffled before by the weight in the air. He began to roam the streets again as he had when he had first arrived, and took a mass of pictures, and looked ahead to the winter and thought how long it had been since he had come there, and wondered if he would spend a whole year in this city.

A postcard had appeared from Laura at the beginning of September. It had been posted a month earlier and it came from Nepal. She said she was living in Kathmandu now so he could stay in the flat indefinitely. *I hope you're getting along with my little gokiburi?* The Japanese cockroaches weren't little at all; they were the biggest cockroaches he had ever seen. She would think it bad karma but he had been setting traps for them since the day he'd moved in. He wrote to Kathmandu that he would keep the flat at least until Christmas. He said, if he was staying so long, he hoped she wouldn't mind if he moved some of her things.

He wrote to Laura and then he took up a second airmail form and wrote to his mother as well. It was the first time that he had written home in weeks but he said nothing about his plans. *The summer was hot,* he wrote. *I went to the seaside. I saw a school of porpoises in the ocean. There are fishing villages in coves by the sea, and the land behind is cut into steep terraces. They grow rice and oranges, and sometimes they grow chamomile. Going up the steep paths I met little old women bent beneath baskets of chamomile on their backs.* He wrote whatever he could write to make the place sound sweet. *I've been taking pictures of gardens.* He looked for the subjects where he could best connect with her. Gardens were one. Too many others were closed. He told how the Japanese gardens lent themselves beautifully to photography, the controlled vistas, the variations in level, the paths that moved through them. Photography in the gardens was about stillness, and angles and depths, stone lanterns and bamboos and maple leaves rising behind. It was quite different from photographing war: no movement, no action, no surprises to it except those that were designed; nothing unexpected. The paths lead you through. In his mother's garden the emphasis was on flowers rather than form, textures and colours and scents. That was because she had been first an arranger of flowers before she was a gardener, and still she grew flowers for cutting, for the house. She had gone to the garden after his father died, as if in consolation or grief she had transferred to herself his father's brooding relationship with the soil. He pictured his mother out in the garden; somehow she always remained neat in the garden, her nails kept trim beneath gardening gloves and her hair carefully arranged, running in as soon as it began to rain with her old brown gardening coat held over her head. There would be a last flush of flowers now before the autumn, yellows and pinks and purples intense in the low light, the first leaves beginning to turn.

The trouble with writing to his mother was that it made him think too much. It brought him back to who he was, to whys and hows and whens. Nothing unexpected, he had written. Yet what did you expect when you went to photograph a war? I don't know why I was surprised, he might have said to her; but a very long time ago he had stopped telling her the things that mattered. She had gone out into the garden alone and he had watched from a distance, from the house or from up in a tree. And now he had gone away almost as far as he could have gone. I shouldn't have been surprised, he might have said. If he had spoken to her. If he had ever spoken to her. If he was to speak to her again. You would have thought that I knew about war. There were dead people. On the ground. In a ditch. A woman lay in a field. I saw her alive before I saw her dead. He wouldn't tell her that, how he saw a body on the ground and blood soaking into the soil. There was that place they would climb to, he and Richard, in the walnut tree at the edge of the lawn, sometimes he would climb up alone and sit astride a branch with his legs dangling and watch as she worked below in the flowers, and words that he might have spoken would form in his head.

A stray lock of hair would fall forward over her temple, and she would stand and smooth it away with the back of a gloved hand.

I met someone else who was there, at the war, he might have said. I don't know what he did there. You can't tell from just looking at him. But you can't tell that about anyone, can you?

His mother said that his father had hated the Japanese. He didn't know if that was true. He didn't know what a man felt who killed people. Did you have to hate someone to kill him? That was what he used to think. His father had hated the Japanese and went to fight them because they were wicked and cruel. And his mother spoke of them with a particular tone of voice which said that they were not forgiven.

He wrote the letters, and went out and posted the letters, then returned alone to his flat. His mother wouldn't buy a Japanese car. His Japanese girl was something else that it was easier not to mention.

I Was There Too

I was there too. I saw you there but you were blind. I think that you were blind in that moment, Jim, that what you had already seen had blinded you. You had seen it happen. I can imagine the start of it. Before the dust and the smoke, before the flames. Before any screams or gunshots. A village going about its morning. Many of the villagers have been up before dawn. The women are carrying water, making their cooking fires, sweeping, in the early mist that hangs about the houses and across the fields. There is the sound of what the women are doing and still there is the sound of the cicada, which has been the dominant sound of the night, but as the sky lightens and the sun begins to rise that sound first intensifies and then it drops, at some particular degree of lightness, and after a moment's silence, an instant of what seems to be deep silence, is overtaken by the sound of the birds and of the frogs, the mass of frogs in the flooded rice fields, as the sun rises and begins to burn away the mist. By then both men and women are going out into the fields to start work ahead of the heat, among them a young mother with the usual conical bamboo hat and a baby tied to her in a sling of bright turquoise cloth, treading the narrow paths raised beside the irrigation channels and between the fields. And into that morning comes the sound of the helicopters, not one but a number of them appearing in the sky like a squadron of vast and vicious damselflies, and those in the fields are running even before the helicopters land. And from the helicopters step soldiers, and you are one of them. And there for me it stops. I can describe that, the scene before, because it is an everyday scene and I have seen others like it, but I cannot describe what it is that happens next, let alone your part in it. You saw the rest. You must have seen it, Jim. You must remember. I did not see until afterwards, and by that time you were blind.

He brought a different girlfriend when they went to the hot spring. She was just as pretty as the last one, a slender girl with the pale skin and long features of an old-fashioned Japanese beauty, and her name was Akiho. This name he would remember; her name and her quiet, and his feeling rather sorry for her. The resort was a remote one up in the mountains and Jim drove them from Tokyo in his car, out on the expressway and then a complicated route cross-country in the dark. Akiho sat with the map in the front seat and the traffic was slow because it was the start of the week-end, and Jim was in one of his moods. He was restrained and cool and silent, and it was all right at first. He drove coolly as he seemed to do everything, but the journey took much longer than they had anticipated, and he was suddenly, unfairly crushing to Akiho when she realised that they had taken a wrong turn. He didn't say much, only, That's taken us way out of our way. The hurt was all in his tone of voice. He turned the car round, abruptly so that his irritation could be felt in the turn, and a little while afterwards when they stopped to fill up with petrol he suggested that Kumiko go in the front instead.

Kumiko can read a map, can't she?

It was Friday night and all of them were tired. Whichever way they went, they wouldn't reach the hotel until very late. They sat a moment silent in the car, Jim standing tall at the driver's door in the whiteness of the petrol station forecourt, his face very fine and tight. Without a word, Akiho got out and went to get into the back, and Kumiko replaced her.

How unkind, Jonathan thought. And then, how alone he is, thinking of him as he had stood in that bright light looking down to them in the dim interior of the car. He is quite alone. I can see that, but the Japanese girls can't – or perhaps they can and that's why they forgive him.

They drove back into the dark and the traffic, skirted a town and found their way up winding mountain roads. For a long time, none of them spoke. Left, Kumiko said. Or, Take the next right. Jim drove smoothly but the tension had not left the car. He took a leisurely hand from the wheel and slotted a cassette in to play. He had picked up whatever cassette he could reach. Dylan. The music should have soothed them. As they turned the bends the headlights moved across the concrete walls of the mountainside. Everywhere along these roads the cut sides of the mountains seemed to be encased in concrete. Jonathan looked out of the window and saw them pass. Dylan drawled on. All there was to see out of the car were the white lines of the road and the engineering about it, the retaining walls and conduits and barriers.

Do you think they really need to do that when they build the roads?

Do what? Jim said. The Japanese girls were silent.

All that concrete? Is it absolutely necessary or is it something peculiarly Japanese? Encasing the mountains and controlling the streams. They do it at the seashore too, they cover everything with concrete. Because of the earthquakes and the volcanoes and the tsunami, perhaps they feel the need to control nature everywhere they can.

I don't know, Jim said. That's a bit philosophical for me. He reached out a hand to the dashboard and switched off the music. Kumiko, why don't you choose a new tape?

There was silence then and he felt foolish for his words. Akiho was asleep or pretending to be asleep. Kumiko chatted to Jim as she took out his tapes and looked through them in the low light that came from the opened glove compartment. He felt excluded, sitting behind, seeing the still back of Jim's head as he drove, his hands negotiating the bends, Kumiko's movements and the curve of her cheek turning towards him as she talked, how prettily she pushed back her hair when he wasn't even looking at her. A signpost loomed up, Japanese characters that he couldn't read. Left here, she said. Then we'll be there. But there was still some way to go. Or it took a long time because the road was slow.

There is only that one photo he has of that day, beneath the umbrella in the rain. They woke late to rain so heavy that you could see the lines of it falling across the darkness of the forest. They went down to breakfast and then lingered over coffee until they thought that the rain had eased enough for them to go for a walk. They borrowed two umbrellas from the hotel, which was all that the hotel had left because other guests had also taken umbrellas, and they went out and took a long walk, on a forest track that wound down into the valley and the village, and in the village they found a place for lunch, but on the way back up the rain was driving and the umbrellas were not enough to keep them dry. This picture he took by the hotel just before they went in. You can see in it that the girls' hair is wet. Jim's hair is wet too, darkened and slicked to his face. He holds the umbrella in his right hand and Akiho stands on his right. Kumiko is on his left, wearing the same red raincoat she had worn before. She has run up to be in the picture and Jim's left hand rests on her waist. He had noticed that as he took the shot.

It was finally said. It was statement and confession and accusation. I was there, he said. This was the moment to say it, if it was ever to be said. This moment at the bath, so still and dim and innocent. It was a dim room like a cave, the bath taking up most of the space, the area around it tiled with dark neutral tiles, and wooden stools and wooden buckets lined up before low taps for them to wash. There was a door and a big glass window to the outside where they could have bathed in the hot spring in the open air – if it had not still been raining so hard – a mist over the spring where the steam and the rain met. They were alone inside, just the two of them naked in the pungent steamy air, Jim squatting and soaping his back and ladling water from the wooden bucket. I was there. His voice came simply against the sounds of water and of Jim's washing. I saw you there. There was a scar on

Jim's back, a livid, jagged scar, and it seemed to tighten as he spoke, as the whole of his back tightened.

It was a raw, recent-looking scar, not one of those childhood scars everyone carries somewhere. He had already been washing when Jim entered the room, coming in with the small white towel held before him. He had noticed at once the beauty of his body like that of some Greek hero, his skin which had a golden tinge to it even where the sun did not touch, the fine golden hairs on his chest; and then when he also crouched down to wash, there was the scar beneath his right shoulder. Jim saw him looking.

'Nam. Looks bad but it was just a surface wound. He soaped across his back.

What was it?

Shrapnel. I was lucky. It just winged me and didn't penetrate.

He poured a ladle of water down himself, soaped himself some more. Beneath him a stream of soapy water spilled across the floor.

We were out in the delta. I'd never been anywhere like it. I guess you might have said it was beautiful if you hadn't of been doing what we were doing there. I guess it was beautiful anyhow. Only sometimes you didn't see that.

I know, he said. I was there.

So simple the words were in the bare room. He spoke them and almost before they were out he saw that long back tense and harden, and all in one moment the wooden bucket was pushed aside and Jim was standing, and he was afraid, with the spilled water running at his feet. He could see that

150

Jim had understood. Perhaps he had remembered, all at once, the memory come back to him of the burning village and how he had fled from it, how he had stalled there at the wall – and the photographer, first standing then crouching before him. Now the position was reversed. It was he, the impassive soldier, who was standing, anger visible all down his body. Jonathan was afraid, physically afraid but he was also afraid of whatever words this man, the soldier, might say, and he was afraid of the memory that surrounded them, that he could feel in his skin, that he seemed to breathe with the wet air. You, the soldier said. The soldier said only that, standing naked before him, and then he stopped. He was suddenly aware, they were both suddenly aware, that two other men had entered the room, two Japanese men muttering to one another in a bass, grunting, male Japanese, coming into the room, finding their buckets and their stools, squatting down to wash, turning on the taps, looking across at them only briefly, turning their eyes discreetly away as if they had come upon some erotic moment, turning the atmosphere in the room from one of anger to one of surreal embarrassment.

The soldier was a soldier no more. He plunged his naked body into the hot water of the bath. He stayed there a long time in the heat, quite still – as long, Jonathan thought, as any man could stay in water so hot. All the time that he was there Jonathan could only wait, squatting on the stool with his head in his two hands, waiting, unable either to leave or to enter the bath so long as the other was in it. And then at last he burst from the water like some wounded whale, and went to a tap and filled a bucket, cold, and emptied it down himself, and shivered.

He stood, holding the little towel.

You took that picture. Do you know what that picture means?

He spoke softly now. At the far end of the line of washing places, the Japanese men were talking to one another and scrubbing themselves with what seemed a perfect Japanese containment.

You go with your camera, you go sightseeing and you think you know what you've seen. But you don't know what war is. You know nothing. That's war, you say. People see your pictures and say, yeah, that's war. They have these words to go with the pictures. That's a soldier in a war. They think they know what that soldier did. They can't begin to know a thing like that. What he did, what he saw, who he is. They see me and they see the rest of it, and they think they know. They don't know what I saw. What I did. They think they know, and they know nothing.

He spoke it all in one low rush, leaning down to him where he sat on the stool, speaking so low that if the Japanese men had understood English they couldn't have caught it. Then he stood to go, and now the bitterness in his voice cut clear across the room. And you. You knew who I was. So what do you want to spend time with me for?

Jonathan got into the bath, slowly, lowering himself into the heat until all of him was immersed but his head. It was good then. Too hot until you were in it up to your neck, then once you were in, it was good. He moved around until he was resting with his back to the other men and his eyes to the window where the rain was still falling onto the spring outside. Rain, steam, water. He tried to think of nothing else. He took a deep breath and closed his eyes and put his hand to his nose, lowered his head for some moments into the bath. When he came out, he poured one ladle of cold water after another down his back.

Kumiko would speak when he went up to their room of the effect of the minerals in the water. She had spent this time at the bath with Akiho. She would say how good her skin felt from the water. He had no sense of that for himself. He saw as if from a distance that she looked very pretty in the yukata she had worn to the bath. Her skin that she said was tingling had a dark freshness to it, a quality like that of the wet pines outside the window. She had opened the window to look out now that the rain had stopped and the mist was lifting, leaning out, her black hair loosely knotted so that it would have fallen in a single movement. There was a stretch of time in which they might have made love before going down to the restaurant for supper. What's the matter? she said. Why so quiet? He stood beside her and saw the mist curl about the trees, the mountains show themselves, and he breathed the smell of the mountains after the rain that was like the smell of her skin after the bath.

Let's go outside, he said. Look, it's not raining any more. So they dressed and went out, and though the rain had stopped drops were falling still under the trees. They came back and took their seats in the restaurant, and Jim and Akiho weren't there. They sat at a table for four and waited a while. I don't think they're coming, he said. I think we should eat without them.

All right, I'll show you. When we get back to Tokyo, I'll show you, if you really want to see.

It had not been enough to tell her that they had quarrelled. He had to say why, and once he had told her why, then she must see the pictures.

I know this man. I cannot believe that he is this terrible man you say. You have to let me see.

I didn't say that he was terrible or not-terrible. I know that the pictures are terrible, that is all.

They spoke about it in the night, and in the early morning when they woke, close but distant from one another, their voices rising higher than was necessary, like bells across the hotel room.

Why do you not want me to see?

Because I wish I had not seen it myself.

It was what you went there for.

Was it?

Wasn't it?

Of course it was. If you go to be a war photographer, you photograph war. That is what you do.

I'm sure I don't know.

He closed his eyes and the words rang through his head again as she got up from the bed and tied her yukata and went to the window, knotting her hair at the back of her neck as she did so, and opening the window wide and leaning out. She had done that before, he thought. So many things you saw you'd seen before; things repeated themselves, came back, again and again; like the pattern of the words they had just spoken, that echoed other words, randomly, a rhyme, some words out of his childhood; things reminded you of other things, any things, from whenever in your life.

The sun was bright on her face, the sky cloudless behind her, the day a very clear one after the rain.

We'd better just go, he said.

They spent a lot of money on a taxi to take them to a station from which they could get a train back to Tokyo. It seemed a great pity to leave that morning when everything was so dazzling, the light and the shade sharp on the road as they went from forest into the open and into forest and out again, the driver taking the bends smoothly as he knew the road well, they sitting in the back seat, apart, each looking out their own side, listening to the smoothly driven car. The bends were tight, the landscape was tight, the mountains small, the views between them narrow, lovely vistas of forest and groves of bamboo and deep ravines, which they must have passed in the dark on their way there, and they could see them now that it was daylight but they had no interest in them any more. Kumiko and the driver had the briefest of conversations, one so simple that even he could follow it, with his basic Japanese and a bit of guesswork. The driver was surprised that they were leaving at such a time, so early on this beautiful Sunday morning. We came with friends, she said, but our friends were called away. Our friends drove back to Tokyo last night. He thought it must seem odd that they hadn't all driven back together – or perhaps it wasn't odd, perhaps it was a reasonable thing that they had chosen to spend the night at the hotel, for which they had after all already paid, and not to leave until the following day. The driver nodded as he raised his eyes to Kumiko's in the mirror. She said how they had thought that they should leave early since they didn't know how long the journey would take. Yes, that was reasonable. The driver nodded again. There were not so many trains, on a Sunday in particular.

They came to the town and the station, and it was a small station on a branch line. They waited almost an hour for a small train that was just two carriages long, and got off it at a big station in a big town, and there was another wait as they changed onto an express, and they reached Tokyo late in the afternoon. He looked out over the expanse of rooftops as they came into the city. It was too soon, he thought. By that time he knew that he had wanted the journey to take longer, to take up all of the day with its immanence, to run on into the night, so that they would not have arrived until so late that she would have had to go home, directly, to be ready for work on the following morning, and she would not be able to come with him out to his flat to see the pictures that she said she must see.

Why don't you go straight home? I can show you some other time.

They sat side by side, subdued. They had not talked much at any point of the journey. The roofs went by them, roofs stretching into the far distance.

No, she said gently. I'd like to see them now.

The buildings got taller about the tracks, closing over them. They were coming in to Tokyo station.

It took quite a while to find the pictures. In one of the few cupboards he had taken for himself was a pile of boxes, prints and contacts and negatives. He had meant, one of those idle summer days, to sort them, but had remained too idle to do more than begin on the task. Wide flat yellow Kodak boxes and green Fujifilm ones, small plastic boxes of slides. A mass of unlabelled negative sleeves. Loose prints, some of them beginning to curl; others in envelopes, named and dated. White envelopes, bigger brown envelopes, some of them bundled together with elastic bands. *Thailand. Thailand beach shots. Temples. Borobudur. Other Java.* Individual strips of negatives slipping to the floor as he took out the envelopes and the boxes, slipping out of them or from between them, he didn't know.

They'll be in one of these.

He pulled out the yellow Kodak boxes, looked for the labels from the Chinese processors, but there were many even of these. Hong Kong was the one place on his travels where he had actually had commercial work, and there were boxes of this, when he looked, pictures he had taken of buildings for a firm of Kowloon architects, of windsurfers for the brochure of a rental shop on Lantau.

I don't know why I keep all of this stuff.

She had made coffee. She stood drinking the coffee, watching.

Can I see some of them?

Look through these. Borobudur. It's beautiful. I was up there a full day, from dawn till sunset. Or I came down, and went back up. A vast stupa itself, and all of it carved, and on top of it a crowd of small stupas like so many meditating Buddhas. Look how the light on them changes through the day, their shadows, the view all round, the view of the volcano that emerges as the sun begins to go down. No, I have them in the wrong order. These are the first ones, very early with the mist breaking, when I first got up there.

Where is it?

You never heard of Borobudur?

But he found it then, in one of the yellow boxes, the magazine. Jim's face stared from the cover.

Here.

She looked. She sat on a cushion before the low table and put the coffee on the table and looked at the cover, and then opened the magazine, smoothing down each page as she turned it, and looked at the pictures inside, and began to read the article that went with them.

*   *   *

Yes, here they all are.

He brought the contact sheets to her where she sat on the floor. Now that she was here he knew that he would show her all of it. He would keep nothing back. He had not intended to do that, he had intended to show her only what had been considered suitable to be published, but this was suddenly a moment in which he could hand it over, all of it, all that had been in his eyes. He knelt beside her at the table. She was still reading the magazine, her two elbows on the table and her hair falling in a curtain about her face. He had first to take away the empty coffee cup, and bring a cloth and wipe the ring that it had made, before he laid out the sheets. He left them on the tatami beside her while he did that, then came back and took them up and placed them across the table chronologically, in the order of their numbered frames. She pushed back the curtain of hair with one hand. The other rested on the magazine, her small careful hand with tapered white-tipped nails, at the edge of the shiny page. He saw that the hand was shaking. It was too late by then. That's the lot, he said. That's everything. I'm sorry, you did say you wanted to see. She had asked to see but he was the one doing the showing; it was his responsibility, not hers. He adjusted the lamp above the spread of pictures. He went to a drawer and took out a magnifying glass, and came back and leaned over her, his hand light on her shoulder, on her black hair, smelling the smell of her and looking over her head as if he were a teacher and she were a child, knowing now that he was doing wrong. He placed the glass on an image some way down one of the sheets, on the first picture that he had taken after the helicopter landed, which was his first imperfect shot of the soldier. When he straightened up he felt dizzy, as if he were standing at the top of a high cliff looking down at a glossy black-and-white sea.

Kumiko had looked at the pictures inside, read the captions on the photographs, and then she had read the piece. She read the horror and then she went back to that picture of Jim on the cover.

He is still there, isn't he? He is still seeing it.

She didn't look up to him though he was standing just behind her, looking down. Perhaps she didn't trust herself to.

He knew what she meant but he didn't answer.

Could that be so?

Perhaps. It happens like that, doesn't it, to soldiers who see wars?

And you saw it?

I just took pictures. I had the camera. I only saw it through the camera. I was there half an hour, an hour, whatever. That was all.

She had not yet begun to view the contacts which he had put before her. She moved now to a kneeling position before the table so that she could bend down across it to see them closely. They were small and it took concentration to make all of them out. She moved the glass along from that first rough shot of the soldier by the wall, into the village, to those confused shots of running people and not-running people and burning houses. Along, from frame to frame. I do not want to see this, she said, yet as she spoke her hand with the glass moved on, mechanically as if it could only go that way and could not be stopped, and she looked at the next. He looked on helplessly. The room was silent except that they could hear light women's voices downstairs. It was Sunday evening, he thought, Mrs Ozawa's daughter came to visit her on Sunday evenings. When Kumiko had got to the end of one strip she went back and started on the strip below it. When she got to the bottom of one sheet, she moved on to the next one.

I shouldn't have done this, he said. I shouldn't have shown you.

But you have.

She did not pause, but went on, the tears falling from her eyes now, onto the glass and onto the sheet. She wiped them away with her hand, wiped the glass on the hem of her sweater when it smudged. Image after image. Moment after moment. Fragments of time that he had experienced, that she was now putting together. She got to the ones he had taken in the fields, the one of the bodies in the ditch – but she did not stop long on that one because it was one of those that had been reproduced in the magazine and she had seen it already – and then the woman on the path.

I think she had a baby, he said. You see, she has a sling to carry her baby in. I looked for the baby but I couldn't find it.

Were you going to take a picture of the baby?

I don't know, he said, and really in that moment he told himself that he didn't. He didn't know why he had looked for the baby or what he would have done if he had found it. Or did he? Would he not have taken the baby's picture as he had taken pictures of everything else? And if it was alive, would he have picked it up, carried it with him, to where, crying in his arms? But there was no crying. He had heard no crying. Then the baby, if there had been a baby, was already silenced. He turned away, and looked out of the window until she was finished with the photos. It was dark and there were lights in the windows of the houses across the gardens, the rectangles of light yellow and soft, and the rounded forms of the bushes showed black before them, and it was quiet, apart from the voices of the two women downstairs, a suburban quiet that somehow only emphasised the vastness of the city that he knew was beyond. There wasn't much more for her to see, if she had got to those ones in the rice fields. Only that last one of Jim, and that too she had seen already. Yet she kept the glass to it for a long time.

Suddenly she stood. Her elbow swept one of the sheets to the floor.

I have to go.

She was halfway to the door. She had gone to take some tissues from her bag – one of those silly little packs of tissues Japanese girls always carried around, printed with cute characters or flowers as if everything in the world must be pretty and nice.

No. Stay a bit. You must stay a bit now.

The tissue was already a wet ball. She fumbled for another. Her eyes and mouth were soft from crying but her voice when it came was hard.

You shouldn't have done it.

No. I'm sorry, I told you that. I didn't want you to see.

Not me, she said. It's not me that matters.

Jim's not guilty. He didn't do anything. He was just sitting there.

He said that, though he didn't know it entirely. He talked. She stood there in the middle of the room with her fingers twitching at the tissues they held and she watched him talk. He knew she was watching though he didn't know if she was listening. Nothing in her expression told him that, though her crying stalled. The table was low between them with the light on the photographs, shining black and white, the fallen sheet in shadow beside the cushion on the floor.

He heard himself telling the story, trying to make it simple. He wanted to apportion blame. Blame this man and not that one, even if they were together, even if the one acted and the other only saw, watched, did nothing, was unable either to act or to prevent the act. A platoon of soldiers. They look the same in uniforms and helmets, all one, running with their guns. The choppers from which they have come not stilled yet behind them, blades just turning. A last piece of dawn hangs in the sky behind the dark outlines of the choppers and the soldiers who come running into the village. The platoon enters the village and what happens, happens. He told the events as he has imagined they occurred, as he has told them to himself, pieced them together from what was said later: how a Viet Cong was caught hiding, or how they caught a young man hiding and this meant to them that he was Viet Cong; how as they held the young man, a boy came out from a hut and threw a grenade and one of their own was killed; and so they killed the man they held, and the boy; and they killed the grandfather who came from the hut to protect the boy; and on and on the killing went; and the burning went on to punish and to cover the killing. The platoon does this, but the platoon is made of individuals. And one individual – or perhaps more than one, perhaps there may have been others, he does not know – runs, at some point in all of this, runs away and puts a wall between himself and what is going on. He sits with his back to the wall, blind to all else.

And then you come and take his picture.

Her voice was plain, stubborn, her figure small and decided. He didn't answer.

She didn't cry any more and she didn't say any more. She went into the hall and got her raincoat and the rucksack, put back the pack of tissues and zipped it up. The sounds she made were efficient, material: the barefoot pad of her steps, the hard brush of synthetic fabrics, the zip, the shuffle as she put on her shoes. White trainers, red coat, black rucksack, out of the door. Running steps down the metal staircase in the darkness to catch her train home.

She had dropped a tissue on the floor. He picked it up and then he picked up the sheets of prints, the one from the floor and then those from the table. The magazine lay beneath them. His words were only a part of the truth. The rest of it was in the soldier's eyes. He put the sheets back into their boxes, and the magazine with them, stacked the boxes with the others in the cupboard and slid the panel back across it, the panel smooth when it was closed, merging with the wall. He could hear Mrs Ozawa and her daughter outside by the foot of the staircase, saying goodbye in soft, light, Japanese women's voices.

It is there in the eyes, in those eyes that make the photograph so effective. The soldier has been inside the village. He has seen, or possibly he has done, whatever it was put that look into his eyes. Is it necessary that he did it, or was seeing enough? Perhaps seeing is guilt in itself. The eyes cannot bear that. They look out pale and shocked and blind from the dirtied hero's face. That's what the viewer wants to believe, that they just cannot bear what they have seen. That this man has been no more than a spectator, a viewer himself. Seeing alone is a kind of guilt, and seeing is shame. Kumiko understood. And you took his picture, Kumiko said, and Jim had said the same thing. Everyone who sees knows the shame.

166

He saw Jim one more time. He saw him as he had first seen him, a golden head above the crowd.

It was at the Omotesando crossing. He saw him just as he came up from underground. It was a chill November morning and the sky as he came out from the station was high and grey, the cars halted, the crowd crossing the road ahead of him in a dark flood.

Possibly he had been on the same train and he had not known it. They might without knowing it have travelled on the same trains all the way from Kichijoji. It was some weeks since since the trip to the hot spring. At first he had half expected to see Jim on the street, as if they were somehow fated to meet up again, as if because they had met before then there was a stronger likelihood that they should meet again. For days, he had avoided the bar; but then he had gone to it, and sat on a stool at the counter and looked for Jim's bottle up there on the shelf, and noted the level in it, and he had gone again a few days later and noted that the level was unchanged, and since then he had not been back. He had no thought of seeing Jim here at Omotesando at this of all times, where so many thousands went on a Sunday morning, where he had gone, idly this November day, to photograph the fashionable and the others among them.

Yet there he was, and it seemed suddenly unsurprising that it was so, his tall figure riding the flood before him. He followed where the flood went. I have done this before, he thought. But if he turns now, he will know me. But Jim did not turn, and besides, there were so many people between them that he need only look down and he would be no one, no more than a paler brown head among the Japanese. It was Jim who could not hide. Jim was visible from a long way off, by his height, his hair, his stride, the length of his legs and that urgency in him that took him always faster than those around him. He gained on the crowd all the time, moving just ahead of the stream up the wide avenue in the direction of the park, and Jonathan kept pace. He might have run. He might without much difficulty have caught up with him, grasped him by the shoulder and made him turn to face him. Look at me, Jim, look at me now. Tell me what you saw. Your eyes, tell me what was in your eyes. But he didn't run. He kept to the same pace, working through the crowd, a second, smaller, browner, figure weaving ahead of the stream. The lights had changed, the traffic was moving again past the pedestrians, four orderly lanes of traffic separated from them by a line of young trees. The trees were almost bare, their branches dark against the pale sky, the last leaves falling through the still air, detached by the morning's cold if not by wind even as the crowd walked beneath.

Somewhere along the way, Jim stopped. He stopped too. When Jim turned into a side street and went into a coffee shop, he waited. He could see Jim inside through the glass of the window, which also held the reflections of the people on the street, saw him behind the passing figures and through the reflections, looking around, going to a table at which a girl was already seated and leaning over to kiss her on the cheek. Then he too was sitting down, leaning towards her across the table, taking her hand. Her face was hidden by her hair. He knew that she would be pretty. She would be pretty like the others. They were lovely, Jim's girls, but they did not stay with him, or he with them. The girls did not last, or it was Jim who did not last, who never let them come close enough to last. That was what you could do with beautiful Japanese girls; you could touch them and yet not be touched, and perhaps, if they were lucky, you had not quite touched them either. It was a kind of transaction that was easiest made between people who were strange to one another. In the coffee shop Jim was rising from the table, Jim who would always be a stranger in this place. He was paying for the girl's coffee though he had ordered nothing for himself. He was waiting while she took her coat from the chair, following her out to the street as she put on the coat, a long camel coat that looked expensive and stylish as she was, watching as she pulled a black coil of hair out from beneath the collar and smiled and shook it smooth.

There was no reason to follow once the girl was there. She tucked a black-gloved hand to the side of his arm and they walked like that all the way up the avenue towards Meiji Jingu, Jim with his hands in his pockets and she with her hand to his arm, though it was only the lightest of touches, and went on across the road to the entrance to the shrine. Jonathan waited, and then he entered too. There was space beyond, grass and trees. He saw them across the grass and stood at a distance from them and took out his long lens. He saw them speak, pause, walk on, apart this time. He could see their hands and their faces but not their eyes. He took no picture. He put the lens back in its case, slung the strap on his shoulder and turned back into the city. He didn't go into the first station he came to but walked on, going nowhere but only into the flood, the streams of men and women passing him, never quite brushing against him, one after another, and not one of them knew him and he knew none of them nor ever would.

6
Girl in a White Dress

K umiko never spoke to him again about the photos. There was just a look the following day, as she sat behind the typewriter in the school reception, that he thought was wholly Japanese. It was Japanese in that he could not interpret it. It was foreign, inscrutable, utterly discreet, all that the Japanese were supposed to be.

He gathered courage, looked at her straight.

Will you come out with me this week?

OK.

She was wearing a prim outfit that morning which held him back, a straight grey skirt and a little red top over a white blouse that was buttoned at the collar. Her hair was pulled tight into a ponytail.

How about Friday?

OK.

What shall we do?

Go dancing.

So they went dancing. They met in Shinjuku and went to a noisy bar, then up in a lift to a disco on a high floor, and they danced and didn't talk. Kumiko wore a red dress and danced like crazy. She looked like a flame in the flashing lights.

He didn't know if something was broken or not. He looked at her face and couldn't tell. She had closed the subject for them both, put it away, folded, perfectly wrapped, the knowledge of his guilt. The Japanese had such skill at wrapping things. Whatever you bought, they took such care to wrap. They made lovely paper and cloths and boxes for the wrapping. They made books with beautiful covers and they covered the covers with brown paper before you took them home. And where there was pain or anger or embarrassment, they wrapped that too, and if you were English you didn't know what they meant, if it was forgiveness or forgetfulness or if it remained between you.

They went hiking again in Chichibu Tama to see the autumn colours, just the two of them now, not four, and in all of that day they did not speak Jim's name. They walked in step, alongside or one ahead of the other, and their feet fell soft on the paths which were already carpeted with layers of leaves.

She looks no different in the pictures he took of her that day in the gorge from the first time they went there. Only the gorge has changed. The colours are all they are meant to be, brilliant reds and golds and a postcard sky. He had taken many of the same vistas as before, vistas that drew others beside himself, who queued (and whom with conscious irony he had photographed queueing) with their cameras at specific points along the path, apparently content to collect the clichés, to store away the same experience that everyone else stored away; and you'd think, when you looked back, that it was the same, the same as before and the same for everyone. Kumiko poses and smiles in front of the waterfalls as others girls do, as families do, as couples or lone hikers do who ask others to take their picture for them. When he compares the autumn photograph with the one from before, he sees that she has posed in front of the waterfalls in the same spot and with the same wide smile as she had posed before. She is the same Kumiko. Only the colour of the view behind her has changed, and Jim is missing, and the girl whose name he fails to remember. It occurs to him as he looks back that the difference he felt was in himself rather than in her. Though it doesn't show. He looks as happy when she takes his picture as the others do in theirs.

He said what everyone said, that the autumn colours were very beautiful in Japan.

Everyone says that, she said.

He wanted to tell her that he came from a greyer place. Sometimes it's like this, he would say, but often it's damp, grey, the colours muted. It was himself he felt muted, pale with doubt.

OK, now I can take a picture of you, she said.

She took the camera from him.

He stood where she had stood, the waterfalls at his back. Too pale, he thought he was, and too far off. A pale gaijin, outside of it all. That was what gaijin meant, someone from outside.

Smile!

Plough

What she did not know with her senses he could not make her know. She knew his body as he knew hers, and beyond that he knew her city but she could know only his words. They went to see an exhibition in the overheated eleventh-floor gallery of a great department store, of Impressionist painting that the Japanese so love; and he showed her a field of plough. It was the best he could do for a city girl, to show what was inside himself. See, he said, how the soil can shine where the metal blade has cut through and turned it up smooth to the light; see, there is purple in its colour as well as brown. They stood on thick carpets hot in their coats with all of the floors of the department store below them, and outside the traffic moving on straight Tokyo streets. What the painting could not show was the feel of it, the weight of plough beneath your feet, hard when it was dry and claggy when it was wet, and the odour, which was less an odour than a sensation of cool air rising, of moisture rising from cut soil that will steam when the sun strikes it after dawn.

His father drives the tractor with slow concentration, twisting his body round to look back as he drives forward, looking at his line ahead and turning too to see the plough draw in the furrows, watching the line of the furrows, the depth, adjusting his pace where the plough skates over a stretch of compacted clay. He watches all that, turning at the wheel, looking ahead and looking back, and seeing the gulls who are his companions following, rising and circling and following again, like pieces of the sky come to the brown land.

His father had committed himself to a tactile world of physical things. To an identity and an existence which should have been so constant and complete that other existences could be forgotten. To an occupation in which a man need never stop, in which work need never be done, which might, you might think, be so physical, so relentless, that it might obliterate all other thought; and yet the mind is there, thinking, while it all goes on, still living its other, previous and continuing life. There is space there for the mind, an emptiness in which thought persists even as the automatic and the physical work goes on. He ploughs the length of a winter's day, and yet there is room in his mind for other thoughts, always, a layer of thought that all the physical work cannot erase, that is turned up again and again, shining like wet clay even as the light fades.

His father had come to the farm after the war. It was his uncle's farm, and his uncle was old, and he came fresh from the army and the East and worked with his uncle and took it on. The work went on there much as it had through the war, with only the changes of modernisation that everyone was making, and those less on this farm than elsewhere because his uncle was old and did not like to see change. He could imagine that the work had gone on in much the same manner throughout all the time that he had been away just as it did now that he was there, and he could trust that it would continue to do so, in his hands or those of some others; that the farm had a permanence not given to other endeavours, that ran through without seam from peace into war and back into peace.

He wished that there was this painting to show her: his father riding on the combine in a cloud of yellow dust; the boys with their mother below in the field, standing in the bright new-cut stubble and seeing the golden crop fall before the header, all in the dust and the roar of it, waving up to the happy man in the stifling cloud and the man waving back, and there was a smile on his face despite the dust, and he shouted something that they couldn't hear but they knew that it was something fine. The painting would be gold as a Van Gogh, happy as a Van Gogh (if Van Gogh were happy), a golden day. Harvest days must by definition be such golden days, when the ripe grain was dry and the sun shone – but then it would be done, and there would be the rest of the year to go round before those days came again, and even as they approached there would be the tensions and fears, the false alarms, the servicing and breaking and repair of unreliable machines, the listening to forecasts and the looking at the crops and the looking at the sky, and the clouding over of the sky, the sudden storms;

and some years, dark days, the flattening of the crop, the heads turning black before they were cut, when the golden days had come only singly through long weeks of rain.

There was his father driving the combine, and the other men out in the field, and the tractor and the grain cart, and old Billy beside them with his gun to shoot the rabbits. He held his mother's hand and watched for the rabbits. Look, Mummy, that one's got away. She tightened her hand on his. Perhaps she was as glad as he was to see the rabbits escape. The roar came close as the combine passed them going back up the field. He thought of the animals hiding in the crop. They were caught in there when the combine came, when it made the first cut around the edges of the field, caught in an island of cover that reduced as the combine worked on, forced further and further into the crop. He thought of their crouching panic, hearing the roar as it got closer and circled about them, until at the last they understood, some of them sooner, some almost too late, that the single strip of safety left to them also would disappear; that they must make a dash for it. When he thought of that, his father was suddenly terrifying, driving in the cloud at the centre of it all, driving the huge red machine that drove the animals out into the new-cut open. Now the combine had reached the end of the field. It turned, worked back towards them. As it approached he saw the heads of wheat shiver as some animal began to make its way through. Something bigger than a rabbit. Might be a hare, he said to his mother. He kept his eyes on the trickle of movement until the animal broke. Look! It ran so close that he could see its fear, dodging this way and that, a hare as big as a dog zigzagging across the stubble. He hoped, desperately, that the hare would get away. He loved Billy at that minute, that he did not raise his gun and let the hare go.

He rode up in the tractor with his father. He sat on his father's knees with his father's arms strong on either side of him and felt the throb of the engine. He could see further from up on the tractor. He could see the fields all round, and the house away across the fields, and the church and the village, and another church in the distance, a dull breadth of land beneath the big sky. He felt power up there. He felt his father's power. He felt safe on his knees with his arms around him, but sometimes he was afraid as well. It was like that with his father. His father was a big man, with strength in him that you could feel. And sometimes the weight of him seemed like a steadiness, but other times there was a tension in him as if he were made of some hard brittle substance and not of flesh, his arms rigid, like straps strapping him in, his mind gone elsewhere, his body hard as if it would break and not bend if Jonathan so much as moved or asked to be released. Even then in the happy golden time, there were moments that went wrong. You did not know when they would come, and that made them the more frightening. There would be sudden anger in him, anger at some fault in the machine or in the field, or at something else never explained, and swear words spat out over the boy's head. He might stop the engine running but keep rigid for some moments as it stilled, as the machine sputtered out a last puff of blue smoke, the boy unable to move from the trap between his arms even as the juddering ceased, the boy putting a soft small hand to his wrist, turning about, asking if they could get down now. And his father would seem to remember him, as if he had forgotten him in all that time that he had been sat between his arms, and help him to climb down.

*T*his was what he thought he had gone to Japan to do: to take pictures of things and of people in their relationship with things. To photograph the material, form without meaning, and somehow achieve meaning in the process. He had photographed tacky modern things, the tasteless or rather the sugary, and the ersatz, where Japan had borrowed from America and Europe – and Disney and pretty much anywhere else – and created its strange new modern material self in the borrowing. And he had photographed beautiful things that seemed imbued with a deep essential identity. No other culture he knew of had given such perfection of beauty to simple things as the Japanese. Perhaps it was his version of his father's physical existence, this absorption in things, even if it was only the seeing and not the doing of them. What he did was to go out early, as the farmer went out early, in the different dawns of different seasons, the almost-empty dawns of summer and the already-populated dawns of winter, and take his pictures, and sometimes he would be taking the same picture as he had taken before but it would be different because this was a different moment. Sometimes the photographs show that, *by the difference in light or by some extraneous feature like a passing figure in summer or winter clothing or an autumn leaf, but sometimes they are almost indistinguishable, and put side by side the repeating photographs will repeat angle and composition as if there was only one way of seeing whatever object it was that was the subject of the photograph.*

Again, there are the tabi, the workmen's shoes, put out to dry on two posts of a bamboo fence, rubber soles and calf-length canvas leggings sticking into the air; yukata hung to dry empty of their wearers; umbrellas in the narrow street below his kitchen window; the old hornets' nest by his door, uninhabited all year but still attached undamaged to the bare hibiscus; the waiting black limousines and the white gloves of sleeping drivers; the station platforms; the rush-hour salary-men on the trains or eating their Morning Service of coffee and slab-toast and hard-boiled egg on stools in cafe windows by the station exits.

He has seen these things too many times. There are just too many images, too many prints, too many negatives, too many rolls of film still undeveloped. And he has brought all of them home. Before he left he knew that he should make a selection but he couldn't do it. He was too close, he thought, he couldn't see his way through. Even now he finds their number overwhelming.

However many there are, he thinks as he looks at them that he has failed. These pictures are not the place. They are only what he had chosen to photograph. They reflect him back to himself. It is not Japan he sees in them but only his failure.

On one of those morning trains he has photographed a girl asleep with her head down and her hair over her face so that she appears to have no face. It's early so there's no one in the seats beside her, there is just this office girl in a belted mac with her hands on the bag on her lap, legs wearing zipped leather boots and angled neatly to one side, catching a last bit of sleep on her way to work. He has taken so many pictures of these people yet still he is not seeing the uniqueness of their identities. He is photographing them much as he is photographing the things. Even when he has been in the city so long, they are collectively Japanese to him. He cannot tell what is and what is not a mask, or catch the moments when the mask slips, those moments that would make a photograph something more than itself. Or perhaps he was asking too much. What he saw were only the neutral faces that the office workers put on so carefully each morning when they woke in the city, in this biggest and most crowded city where there must surely be more office workers than in any other city, or when they woke outside of the city in whatever distant suburb they lived, the faces they put on when they were half asleep before the long journey which they would make like sleepers, sleepwalking their way into work, sleep-walking through the crowds but with a mask of wakefulness that was dignity for themselves and politeness to everyone else.

The Japanese that he had learned was not enough. He had become accustomed to watching others speak without the expectation that he would understand. He watched as an outsider, watching their speaking mouths and their eyes and their hands, and whatever were their surroundings when they spoke, as if it was all of equal value.

Knowing what he did of the language, he would make out individual words that he understood, but beyond that he listened only to the pattern of it, and Japanese was full of pattern, of the repeated sounds that marked the points in a sentence, of the repeated words of courtesy, of small unimportant words that were used again and again as if they were only the beat in the slow dance that connected one speaker with the other.

Sometimes since he had been travelling he longed to be home where he knew what it was that people were saying. Sometimes he feared terribly the time that language would again close in on him. To be foreign was an attempt to be abstract, to free himself of the baggage of meaning.

He went out alone, pushing himself to see more, to see more closely, to see what was beneath. He experimented with photographing what his eyes saw but his mind didn't recognise, the unformed moments, sights that didn't register because they had no significance: the tap running, the telephone ringing but the photograph is silent, the car that passes though it will appear still in the picture, a chair leg, the ground at his feet, the white lines of an empty pedestrian crossing, a tangle of electricity wires and then a pigeon in a blur above his head; then lowering his camera he took a picture of the obvious, a flat display of sunglasses in a shop window, ranks of paired black eyes staring out into the street.

He went back underground. This project he hoped might be the most successful. The people underground are composed. They walk at a constant pace. They know their

185

position on the platform, which exit they will take from the platform where they get off to make a transfer or to go above ground. They queue in a line just where the doors will open. Nothing interrupts their composure. The station guards with their white gloves oversee their steps, and only occasionally do they intervene or change the pattern, only in the rush hour when they become important, conducting, directing, packing the people into the trains. And the trains move off, people pressed inside against one another and against the glass of the just-closed doors.

Then there is a series of the little trees in the garden at Kamakura, where he had tried to capture the delicate contrived aesthetic that was alien to him and yet meant so much to the old man. He had crouched and then lain on the ground before the pots and angled the lens into their branches in an attempt to alter their scale and portray them as trees from nature, but that defeated their essence. Their identity was all in the artificiality and the metaphor, the microcosmic story they told of the wild within the civilised confines of the garden. So in the end he took the series like portraits in the low autumn light, each tree with the old man beside it, its scale clear, its height even in its pot no greater than that of the wheel of his chair, that low sharp light having the same value on its bark and on its needles or dying leaves as on the old man's skin and his hands. Later he would look them all up in a book so that he could caption each portrait with the name of the species and the style, names which the old man had given them in the garden but which

he had failed to catch at the time. Elm, juniper, cypress, pine.
Chokkan, kengai, sekijoju, sabamiki.

So, you've come to see the hydrangeas.

He was lucky. It was one of the old man's good days. He remembered the British boy and spoke to him in simple Japanese that a British boy could attempt to understand.

You are too late. The hydrangeas are finished.

He bowed, replied with as much respect as his command of the language permitted. It's your garden, sir, I'd like to see. I have my camera. I would like, if you would allow me, to take some pictures of your trees.

Then push me, if you would be so kind. I will show you round.

They moved him into a wheelchair and put a woollen hat on his big bony head, and tucked a blanket round him, tight beneath his arms and over his knees. They pulled the doors wide and Jonathan wheeled the chair, awkwardly as he had not wheeled anyone in a chair before, down the ramp that had been placed to allow him to go into the garden, and made the tour with him, slowly past the groups of bonsai in their pots.

That's a tree in a wind, he said.

He talked a surprising amount. His eyes were bright with his rare alertness and with the cold. He spoke all those names, spinning into incomprehensible detail as he elaborated the methods by which each branch and twig had been bent and trained and pruned in imitation of specific conditions of nature: the tree whose branches had been swept all in one direction as if by the wind, the one whose roots had been made to grow like tentacles about a rock; the *sabamiki* pine, whose trunk had been ruthlessly split down the centre as if struck by lightning.

This pine is most beautiful in winter. You must come back in the winter and see how the snow rests upon it.

Certainly I shall. But I like to take pictures of them now, in this autumn light. This maple, for example, the red of this maple is particularly beautiful right now.

All of them are beautiful in the snow. The snow covers everything, you know.

He waved his hands about and the blanket slipped off him, and Kumiko who walked behind picked it up and settled it around him again and straightened his hat, as Jonathan took out his camera and took pictures.

They went on down the path to where the shrubs were and where the taller trees stood over their heads, and the path became thick with fallen leaves, the leaves heaped up in places so that it became hard to wheel the chair. Kumiko suggested that before they left they might sweep up the leaves so that it would be easier to pass, but her grandfather said, No, don't move the leaves. He spoke suddenly with a kind of urgency or even fear – or perhaps it was no more than an old man's irritation. No, don't move the leaves. They cover the ground.

And Jonathan suddenly thought, he's afraid of the soil. He too has seen blood in the soil and knows that the soil smells of blood.

He wheeled him on very gently and took care that he did not disturb the leaves, and other leaves fell as they went and there seemed to be a softening in the air and on the ground, and the woollen hat lolled as he dropped off to sleep in his chair, and it was hard to pull the chair back up the ramp without waking him.

Again, the train, the roof-scape. Both of them silent at first, then Kumiko spoke.

Do you know what he said to me? Did you understand all that he said?

I understood pieces of it, only pieces. Words, the names of the trees, not the rest of it.

He said to me, It doesn't matter if I catch cold. Did you notice? He didn't want me to put the blanket on him? I think he dropped the blanket on purpose. He said he did not want to live beyond the winter. He did not want the spring to come round again, or the rainy season or the summer.

The view from the train was beginning to be broken now. They were coming to the tall buildings of central Tokyo. It was getting dark but it wasn't dark enough. Sometime he meant to travel one of these lines into the city at night and take a long exposure of the lights, a horizontal blur of lights massing as the train moved on into the centre.

A long panoramic shot. Rails, tarmac, concrete, roofs, the sky black above, the lights streaking below the sky. The city covering over all of the soil.

What's the Use?

Before he left for Asia he had taken a series of photographs of the farm. It was the end of the summer. He had been home for a few weeks to help his brother with the harvest, and when it was done they burned the stubble. He had taken pictures of the stubble burning. They had ploughed the headlands first. They had ploughed a few times around the edge of the field so that the fire when they lit it would be contained and not burn out the hedges. They had worked on a day when there was only a fine breath of wind, a crystalline September day. They had watched for the strength and the direction of the wind and then seeing that it was safe they set light to the field, at the end into the wind, and saw the stubble catch and crackle, gold to flame to smoke moving across the field, a narrow belt of fire, the smoke rising grey and turning white as it massed and spread, the ground bared and black where it had passed. In the distance they could see where other fields were burning, distant patches of red and smoke rising from fields other than their own, smoke spreading white into the sky, and all the air in the countryside was sharp with the smell of burning. He took pictures of the whitened sky above and the charred land below, and the flames in the stubble and the smoke welling up, images that if you closed in on them appeared to show the earth itself on fire.

What's the use of that? his brother said. Richard had his gun with him and shot a big rat that was running from the fire. The rat was fat from feasting on dropped grain. He picked up the spent cartridge but left the dead vermin where it lay. You might do something useful, instead of farting around with a camera.

*T*he pictures show time broken into pieces. He can arrange them to reconstruct all of his time in Japan. First, the ones he thinks of as the tourist shots: the sights, the Imperial Palace, Ginza, the Asakusa Temple, Meiji Shrine, and then the first of streets and the underground. Kumiko beneath the wisteria. More streets, and more of the underground. More of Kumiko, many of Kumiko, a whole boxful of Kumiko, her face, her lips, her smile, her eyes. The pieces of her body that he loved. Along with those, in the chronology he puts together, come the garden pictures and the rain pictures and the summer pictures. Many of these last are in colour. On the streets the signs and the colours can seem lurid beneath the haze of the polluted sky. On trips outside Tokyo, the greens are intense, the skies strong, Kumiko in her summer clothes bright in the foreground. (When she is naked she looks most beautiful in black and white, but a soft, matt, slightly grainy black and white which brings back to him the lovely but imperfect texture of her skin.) As the summer goes on, Jim appears. He had taken many more photographs of Jim than he had realised. Jim made such a striking figure on the streets. Perhaps he was instinctively using him as a foil, *his figure so effectively set off the Japanese-ness of the rest. And sometimes there is a visible tension between Jim and the rest that has the effect, he thinks, of projecting into the picture his own foreignness, the relationship he himself has with the city that he is trying to portray. But perhaps he was photographing Jim just because he was handsome, or because somehow he had come to love him. Some of these shots are good, if he were to show them, if he were ever to use pictures of Jim again. An* American in Tokyo, *he would call them, and they would tell their own story, the glamour, the looks of the girls, the stride, the aloneness. But he will not allow himself to use him. Not Jim, not again, it would not be fair to use him again. He works on through the other summer pictures, yet none seem so satisfying. He moves on to later, bleaker ones, when he isn't seeing Jim any more and when Kumiko is so often gone to Kamakura and he is spending more time alone in the city as he had at the start, and though these pictures are in many ways similar to those he took at the beginning he thinks that perhaps they are getting closer to what he wants. He finds the ones he took that day in Omotesando, many of which at first glance almost repeat those he took in Omotesando in the beginning, yet the subjects of the pictures have shifted just so slightly, to the ordinary, the unselfconscious, the inadvertent, the flawed, alongside the self-consciously created images of the fashionable. Among these he finds his last picture of Jim, just the back of his head above the crowd. He remembers standing in the park watching Jim and his girl through the zoom, but it seems that he took no pictures at all through the zoom that day. It comes back to him, how instead of taking pictures he had only watched, and the sadness*

he had felt for Jim and for the unknown girl and for himself,
and then how he had put the lens back into its case, slung the
strap on his shoulder and turned away into the city through
the sea of Japanese, and how he seemed to himself then to be
passing through the alien city like a diver underwater, breath-
ing his own oxygen that he carried with him, that was not the
surrounding air.

The Gun Room

Gun room was a grand name for it, a name suggestive of bigger houses and other times. The place where his father kept his guns was little more than a cubbyhole opening out from his study, a crooked oily-smelling space beneath the stairs with room in it for a workbench and a stool, and leather gun cases and cartridge belts and other bits of shooting paraphernalia, besides the metal gun cupboard fixed to the wall, and a tiny narrow window that shed light across his father's face where he sat with the gun on his knees. The metal cupboard was open, the thin light on that too, on the dark gleaming barrels of the three guns that stood upright in their rests, and on the empty space where the fourth had been removed. There was nothing strange about his father having taken a gun down yet the moment was strange. What was strange was the way his father looked.

He had gone into the study only to borrow something from the desk, a pencil or a ruler or something like that. He was only going to the desk to borrow whatever it was from amongst the usual mess of papers, his father wouldn't have minded him doing that, and he glanced to the side and saw his father there in the gun room, and he stood a moment and looked, and ran out of the study without it, whatever it was. His father was just sitting looking ahead of him, looking into the study, looking directly at him but not seeing him. At least, he thought that he did not see him, and certainly there was no suspicion or mention of it later. His father was sitting on the stool beside the bench where he kept his things for cleaning the guns, but he had swivelled the stool round to face into the study and sat with the gun held flat across his lap, his two hands on the stock and the barrels, cupping its length in his hands like a power. Daddy/I'm sorry/I just/I want/Have you got ... There were words that it would have been easy to say, but he said nothing. Words would have broken the moment. He stood for that split second and then ran out, closing the door very softly behind him. And he never forgot.

The pose wasn't the same as Jim's. Jim had crouched on the ground with his knees up before him and the gun held vertical between them. Jim's face was dirty with war, his father's clean in the winter light. But the look in their eyes was the same: frozen, blind with what in Jim he thought was shock, but in his father it must have been memory, or intention. Past, or future.

*   *   *

Do Japanese farmers have guns?

There was Jim holding a gun, his father holding a gun.

I don't know, she said. I don't know any country people.

In England all farmers have guns.

He took that picture of Jim because he had already that picture of his father, the two pictures merged now by some chance double exposure, the one above or beneath the other.

Some Japanese people go hunting, she said. I think maybe people go hunting but I don't know anything about it.

We don't call it hunting, we call it shooting when we go with guns. Hunting's what you do with horses.

In a red coat?

That's right.

I've seen pictures, men in red coats chasing foxes.

Their conversation became light. Everything became lighter once he was with Kumiko. Her smile didn't show only in her mouth but there could be a small one, just a sense of a smile, in her eyes first.

English farmers have guns for shooting rabbits and pigeons and pests.

Japanese people think rabbits are cute.

So do English people. Farmers don't think they're cute because they eat the crops.

And what about foxes?

Foxes eat the chickens.

Her smile was broadening now. He was sitting on the edge of her desk in the office, looking down at her. There was no one there but themselves. They were about to leave. He had been teaching English all day and here he was having an inane conversation like one in an English lesson, full of unnecessary sentences, question and answer and repeated structures and related vocabulary.

Do you have a gun? she asked him.

My brother has guns. He told her about his brother. My brother has my father's guns.

Guns, plural, that means he has more than one. See how I work in a language school. How many does he have?

Three. There's a .410, which is a lightweight gun that boys can use, then the 12 bore, then the 16 bore. There was an old and valuable one that used to be my great-uncle's, before, but my brother sold that one. When he says 'before' his hand points behind him. It is an English teacher's habit, to point back when you mention a thing in the past, to point forward when you mention a thing in the future. It helps the student to identify tenses, and to keep track of all those little words in a sentence that can indicate time.

They went out from the office, down in the lift.

I saw Jim yesterday.

Where?

In the street. I didn't speak to him, I just saw him.

You should have spoken to him. Those things are meant, when you see people like that.

They went to a yakitori bar. They were going to eat quickly and then go to the cinema.

The trouble is, you're a Pisces, she said. You're bad at taking the initiative. You see and you don't act.

She asked what Jim's star sign was and he said he had no idea.

Only the Dog

What was there that he could have done? Only spoken. He could have run back and spoken then – or screamed, rather, screamed as he ran across the plough, stumbling on the hard-frozen clods, running home, and nobody would have heard him out there in the fog but Billy, and Billy had heard the shot already and was already by then on his way to the spinney. He could have called the others out, when he got to the house, shouted from downstairs, or run up and hammered on their doors, and brought them out, his mother and Richard in their night clothes running through the fog, the fog beginning to thin by the time he had got them outside, concentrating itself into a milky streak along the ground, the sky above beginning to clear with a thin white sun showing through.

Then they would all three of them have seen, standing over him on the leaves, his mother's hair wild that normally she kept so neat and her nightdress sticking out from under her coat, and Richard with his pyjamas spilling over the tops of his gumboots. And maybe, seeing them, the dog would have stopped its whining and come over to them, to the rest of the family standing shivering there, come over, sleek and dark from the damp, and rubbed against their legs and their cold knotted hands. But they didn't get to see, only the dog saw, and the dog came to them later when they sat all three of them together on the sofa, and was warm then and nuzzled them, and he looked at its brown pools of eyes and slobbery mouth and pink tongue, and he might have spoken then but he didn't. He bent towards the dog. He rubbed its ears and put his head to its smelly golden coat that smelled of dog but also of the earth and the blood and the leaves, and he knew that Richard was looking at him. There was a great black chasm between them from that moment, between himself and Richard, and between himself and his mother too. Because of what he and not they had seen.

It was a lie, what she told them, between them on the sofa. He knew that it was a lie.

It was foggy that morning. No one goes out shooting in the fog.

And his father was in the spinney, not the field. There was no fence in the spinney. There had been no accident, no climbing of any fence.

*T*his picture he did not take, of the girl in the white dress, yet he sees it as if he had taken it, a single still shot that will be followed by a blur too fast for his eyes. Here, in England, in the little-used dining room of the farmhouse, where the yellow and the green boxes are variously spread and stacked on the carpet, and the pictures piled on the long oak table, he goes to the window and looks onto the wet lawn and the bare trees of winter, and he sees the image sharp, clear as the glass of the window and the empty view.

He has brought home few things besides the boxes of photographs and undeveloped rolls of film, only a suitcase of clothes, and Christmas presents for his mother and for Richard. He had taken time on the presents and Kumiko had helped him buy them, a red lacquered bowl for his mother, and for his brother a tool of a type seen and admired at her grandfather's, a folding prun-ing saw of high-quality Japanese steel, the handle of hardwood shaped with a tactile and oriental-seeming curve, but then at the last moment he couldn't think of Richard doing any pruning *except with a chainsaw, so he had bought in addition a bottle of some expensive Japanese whisky. He thinks that they liked the presents. They seemed to understand that he had taken care with them. How long will you stay for? they said, and he said, Till after Christmas anyway. That's fine, they said, stay until you're sorted out. You can use the top bathroom as a darkroom again, as you used to, some of your things are still up there in the attic. And have the dining room to sort your pictures – not over Christmas of course, we'll have to have it clear for Christmas, but in the meantime, and afterwards, if you're still here. You know how little entertaining we do nowadays. It's much more friendly anyway to have people to eat in the kitchen.*

His mother looks older. That had struck him forcibly when he got out of the taxi and she came to the door. But then he had understood that the impression was partly an effect of the falseness of memory, that the memory which he had been keeping and against which he had measured her most likely dated from some time long before he had left. (From what age should you keep a memory of someone, he wonders, at what age would you take their portrait, if you were to keep of them just a single portrait, as the Japanese do, for the family shrine?) All in all, she looks well enough. It must help that Richard is running the farm so efficiently now. As for Richard, he seems fine, unchanged, except that he appears to respect him a little more. They were great, those Vietnam pictures, he had said. It is almost the only praise he can remember having from Richard. Why didn't you go on with it? Their mother says that Richard needs a wife, a girlfriend at least, and then he sees her look on himself, the question in her, and volunteers nothing.

203

Later she will see the pictures of Kumiko – some of them,
those that he will allow others to see. The photographs might be
assembled to make a story but it won't be the right one. It won't
ever be the full story because of all the images that are missing.

Is a man responsible for what he sees, or only for what he looks at? He has read that somewhere, someone asking that question. Did he look at this girl on the platform, or only see her? If he had had his camera in his hand, would he have taken her picture?

He was waiting for a train on one of the suburban overground lines, heading out of the city centre while the commuters were heading in. It was one of those mornings when you could see Fuji. The first time he had seen Fuji from this station he had missed a train in order to take a photograph, so rare the sight seemed, so magical the cone of the mountain rising disconnected above the city. He had not known that it would become a recurrent sight on clear days in winter. This particular Wednesday morning was bright and cold, and Fuji was there on the horizon, and he noticed the girl because she wasn't wearing a coat. She wore a white dress, no coat, but she did not look cold. The dress was tight at the waist, the skirt flared out to the calf. It was the sort of dress in which it would have been lovely to see a girl dance. She might have worn the dress to go out the night before, be returning home now without her coat after a wild night out and a one-night stand, but she looked too pure for that. She stood at the fore of the crowd of waiting passengers on the opposite platform, standing very still, but then they most of them stood still, they were people waiting, living the blank moments, the dead routine of their day. Just the hem of her skirt fluttered with the breeze that came down the open space of the tracks. So many times he had stood like this and watched the people waiting, photographed the figures and the patterns they made, composing his picture perhaps around the one element that stood out, a child or a particularly dapper man or a bright shopping bag, taking another picture as the crowd shifted and the element moved.

She stepped out like a petal detaching itself from a flower. His eyes were on her. He did not see but only heard the oncoming train. The sound. The rush of air. The screech of the train braking. The gasp of the crowd which took away his breath, took away all of their breath so that for an instant there seemed to be no air in the place at all but only metal.

There was nothing more. Whatever there was, was swept away at the front of the train. There was only the crowd, acting as one, moving back, moved back like a wave by the men in white gloves, like a wave pulling back from a beach, pulling back with a strange slow calm though you could see the shock and the hysteria on individual faces, streaming out through the turnstiles, out of the station into the street, breaking up there, milling about, then gathering again at the bus stops along the road to have buses take them to wherever it was they wanted to go.

* * *

He was late for the lesson but that wasn't a problem. His student was a housewife whose life seemed too small for her and whose dream was to travel to Europe. She didn't mind that he was late and the lesson went surprisingly normally. He had done his preparation and the student had done her homework. They read a passage about Italy and talked about what a Japanese tourist would like to see there, the Vatican and the Bridge of Sighs, and Michelangelo's *David*, and he kept his concentration all through. When the lesson was over, he went to a public telephone and made an excuse that he was ill, cancelling his teaching in the school that afternoon. Then he went to a coffee shop and sat in it for a long time. By the time he went home trains were running from the station again, precisely to schedule.

He went back over his pictures. Prints, contacts, negatives. He sorted through everything he had of the underground. He had dozens of that station. They were his Wednesday-morning pictures. It was a good station for pictures because of the views from the platform which was raised above street level, and the Wednesday lessons were well timed for going against the crowds. He put aside all the pictures he thought he had taken at that station and then went through them with the glass looking for the girl.

Sometime late in the afternoon Kumiko came by. He opened the door to her.

Are you OK? I called, I kept calling, and you didn't answer. You said you were ill. Are you ill? She touched his forehead to feel his heat. You don't look so ill, but you don't look well. What's the matter?

He let her in. I'll make some coffee, he said, and let her walk through into the room.

What is it? What are you doing? Why didn't you come to work? She was getting angry, seeing all the pictures. I thought you were ill. I had to find replacement teachers. What's going on?

He told her what he had seen.

She sat down on the floor then, began to pick up the pictures from the table. And what are you doing?

I was looking for her. I wondered if I had seen her before.

Are you crazy?

She started to cry. Perhaps that was what he needed to do, to cry.

Are you completely mad? Do you know how many girls there are in Tokyo?

I think I have to go home, he said.

He could not bear it. He could not bear that he was only a witness. That all he could do was watch. He could not bear her foreignness. She, all of them, were foreign to him, all of them on the other platform, even Kumiko was on the other platform, over the tracks, observed by him but not to be touched by him, not to be touched or saved if he might have had the chance to save her.

I can't explain. It's just that I'm outside of all this. I can't live all of my life outside.

Like Jim, she said. Kumiko was always wiser than he thought.

Yes, I guess, like Jim.

Jim could not go home. I think that he could not go home because of your picture. But you can go home.

Then I have to, don't I?

He might be outside at home too, but he couldn't tell her that. Only that he needed to be there.

*T*he dining room is dark because it had been decorated for evening circa 1958, decorated by his mother with deep red walls and chintz curtains. It would be a dark room anyway because the windows are low and north-facing. He has lights on even in the daytime, the wall sconces and the desk lamp that he has brought in to put on the table, plugged into an extension lead that runs across the floor. You need a lot of light to look at pictures.

Call me, she had said, but he will not call. He is afraid to call, for fear that her voice will be too small and strange to him, more foreign, more Japanese, than he remembers. He fears the distortion, the echoes that can occur down the international line. He will write instead and ask her to write back. He believes that he will hear her voice more clearly if she writes to him.

I'm having a show. I want you to see it. He has been trying to make his selection dispassionately, objectively, ruthless as when he looked through the lens. None of the underground pictures are

209

innocent to him now. Not one of them, not one of those bland figures is bland any more. He is aware of the potential in each and every one. They are walking through halls and tunnels, up stairs and down escalators, walking down on to the platforms of the various lines below ground or up to the platforms of other lines above ground, and all the platforms end the same way; they come to an end all of a sudden in a straight line and any one of those people lined up before the line might step over the line. And they wait for the train to come. And the instant before the train comes there is a rush of air. I'm getting a show together on the underground. Nowhere famous, just a gallery in north London, but it's a start. Floating, I'm going to call it, floating like in ukiyo-e, like in the old pictures of Japan that people know, but like in Buddhism too: the floating world of the city but the sadness as well.

He will go outdoors and take a picture for her. I never showed you my home. Here it is. Come and see me. See how it is here.

The picture he sends her must be colour. Kumiko loves colour. It should be a flowery picture. She likes his pictures of flowers best. They say it's flat here and grey and often that's true. It's always flat but he has told her that sometimes it's golden. That's at harvest time. Right now the fields are still brown, but not the garden. The garden has the beginnings of new green, and flowers. In the garden the daffodils are coming out, yellow not gold, a flood of yellow that when they are fully out will stretch from the old sycamores all the way to the house. That will be the perfect English image for her. His Japanese students have been given Wordsworth to read at school. They know Wordsworth like they know Van Gogh. Kumiko will surely have read the Wordsworth. When she comes, if she comes, perhaps he will take her on a trip to the Lakes.

He will wait for the flowers to come out and then he will set up the tripod facing back through the trees to the house. Stand in the daffs, feeling silly – looking it too, at least to an English eye. Set the self-timer, run back to his spot, reach out his arms and smile.